Other books by E.B. Wheeler

The Haunting of Springett Hall
Born to Treason
No Peace with the Dawn (with Jeffery Bateman)
The Picture Bride (in *The Pathways to the Heart*)
Yours, Dorothy

Letters FROM THE Homefront

E.B. WHEELER

Rowan Ridge
Press

ISBN: 9781729298343

First printing: October 2018

Published by Rowan Ridge Press, Utah

Cover and interior design © Rowan Ridge Press

Front cover photos ©Taras Atamaniv, ©Didgeman, ©GregMontani
Back cover photo of Bushnell General Military Hospital courtesy of Otis Historical Archives, National Museum of Health and Medicine

To the patients and staff of Bushnell Military Hospital,

1942-1946.

Your sacrifices are not forgotten.

Chapter One

A BRILLIANT DECEMBER SUNRISE painted the snow atop the Wellsville Mountains shades of rose and tangerine, but Evie didn't have time to enjoy the view.

"Some other day," she promised herself, her whispered words forming a white cloud in the chill air.

She forced her gaze to stay on the sidewalk and not admire the mountains. The Utah-Idaho Central streetcar had dropped her off on 500 West, so she was five blocks from Main Street and the shuttle bus to Bushnell General Military Hospital with not much time to get there. She scurried past quiet brick houses with darkened Christmas trees in their windows.

The hospital would already be stirring: The Stars and Stripes snapping bravely in the frosty air, the huge steel ovens in the kitchens firing to life, yawning doctors and nurses buttoning on crisp, white coats. Evie had to be at her desk on time, ready to do her part to save American lives and defeat the Nazis and their Axis allies.

A train to the west puffed its white breath into the predawn air. Its horn blast broke the morning stillness as it roared along the tracks from the Union Pacific depot toward the hospital snuggled against the foothills to the east. More new patients arriving: young men missing arms and legs, carried in on stretchers to their last, best hope of returning to some semblance of their lives before the war.

The courthouse clock chimed the half hour, and Evie clutched her handbag and broke into a jog down Forest Street, the cold air stinging her throat. The breakfast scents of bacon and ham from the Idle Isle Cafe beckoned her, and she rounded the corner onto to Main Street.

An iron arch over the road proclaimed, "Welcome to Brigham City." Evie paused to catch her breath. Another woman stood at the bus stop in front of the three-story, brick facade of the Howard Hotel, so the shuttle would be sure to stop. Evie crossed the road and passed dim storefronts festooned with garlands and announcements of Christmas bargains.

A large poster jarred the festive decorations with its reminder: *Loose lips might sink ships. Enemy spies are everywhere.* Caricatures of Adolf Hitler and his ally, Japanese Emperor Hirohito, leered at Evie from the poster. She shuddered and turned up the collar of her coat.

The woman at the bus stop looked up when Evie approached and gave her a pale smile. The woman wore a colorful scarf covering most of her dark hair and cradled an enormous belly under her knee-length wool coat. Evie had left college after one year to work at Bushnell and help with the war effort, but this woman looked even younger than her—barely eighteen, if that.

"Morning," Evie said.

"Good morning," the other girl said with a weary smile.

Evie gestured to the newly-installed bus stop bench. "You should sit."

The girl gave the bench a longing glance. "It says it's for the patients at Bushnell."

Evie laughed. "If any of them are out this early, they'll be court-marshalled." She sat primly on the edge of the bench and patted the spot next to her. If it was just her, she would not have dared sit there either, but the pregnant girl needed to rest.

The girl smiled shyly and slipped onto the bench next to Evie.

"I only hope I don't break it. I feel as big as an elephant."

"I bet you're just a wisp of a thing under that coat," Evie said. "Are you headed to Bushnell?"

"Yes. My husband's recovering there. We got permission for me to have my baby at Bushnell so I can be close to George. My name's Jeannie, by the way. Jeannie Harding."

"Evelyn Lewis. It's good to meet you."

"And you're going to the hospital as well? Are you a nurse?"

"Nothing that grand. I'm a medical secretary. I take notes for the doctors and type them. Sometimes I talk with the patients to cheer them up."

"That's important too."

Evie smiled with a glimmer of pride, but the practical part of her mind scolded her with a reminder that she was a very small cog in the giant war machine. The flush from her jog was wearing off, and the trickle of sweat on the back of her neck turned cold in the icy air. She shivered and adjusted her coat, putting her gloved hands under her arms to keep them warm. "We all have to do our part."

"I'm glad you do. When George was injured..." Jeannie's eyes grew distant and dull.

"Was he at Normandy?" Evie asked, carefully gauging the size of Jeannie's belly for a guess at when George must have left.

"Oh, no. That's the funny thing. I was so relieved that he missed it. I thought the war was practically won, and he'd be out of danger for sure. And then there was a training accident back east. He's lost his leg. I haven't seen him yet." Jeannie's face turned a paler shade of alabaster.

Evie touched her shoulder. "He's at the best place in the world for that. Wait until you see our boys. They learn to dance and play baseball and even drive cars. Your George will be back to himself in no time."

As long as he wasn't one of the battle fatigued ones in the NP: the neuro-psychological ward. Their vacant stares were enough to give Evie goose prickles, as though they couldn't tear away from the ghosts of the battlefield that had followed them home.

Evie put on a bright smile. "Did you just arrive in Brigham City, then?"

"Last night," Jeannie said. "I got off the train in Ogden, not sure where to go. A nice woman asked me where I was headed, and when I told her Brigham City, she offered me a ride. We got up to the USO ladies' housing office, and they said there wasn't a bed left in Brigham City, not even room on the floor somewhere! They told the woman who gave me the ride that I was her problem. It was too late to go to the hospital. She took me home and put me in her bed, and she slept in her kitchen. Can you imagine? She already has guests in every room in her house."

Evie smiled. "No room in the inn. Are you sure your husband's name isn't Joseph?"

Jeannie blushed rosy pink. "You're teasing me!"

"I am. But Brigham City is overflowing now that Bushnell is here. They squeezed me into a room in the hospital quarters with another girl, so I usually don't have to worry about the bus, but I spent the weekend visiting my little brother. He works at the Defense Depot down in Ogden."

"I'm surprised he's not..." Jeannie bit her lip as though afraid she might have said something offensive.

"He has a medical deferment," Evie said quickly. She didn't add that it was her fault that he was crippled, unfit for battle.

"What do you think you're doing in that seat!" came a sour, wrinkled up voice from behind them.

Evie jumped to her feet to stare down at a woman whose face perfectly matched her voice.

"That seat's for soldiers only." The sour-faced lady stabbed at Evie with her umbrella.

Evie put a hand on Jeannie, who was struggling to rise. "This lady is a soldier's wife, and she'll soon be a maternity patient at the hospital. She has every right to sit here."

"It's okay," Jeannie said timidly. "I'll stand."

"No, you stay sitting. Take care of your husband's baby." Evie glared down at the old woman, who glared right back.

The shuttle's arrival saved them from a showdown. The little, tan bus rolled to a stop and the doors hissed open. The sour woman pushed past both of them to hobble up the stairs. Evie helped Jeannie to her feet and guided her onto the bus. The sour woman had taken the first available seat, so they shuffled a bit farther back, past doctors, nurses, and family members going to the hospital. Evie relaxed in the relative warmth of the bus. She would be on time to work.

When Jeannie sat down, though, her face was porcelain white.

"Are you okay?" Evie asked.

"I'll be fine. I didn't get breakfast because I didn't want to wake Mrs. Anderson—the nice woman who took me in."

Evie opened her handbag, where two Milky Way bars hid in a side pocket, their green lettering bright on the white wax paper wrappers. One for her, and one for her older brother Albert when he got home from the war. They were his favorite, but he had always kept one ready to share with Evie and Robbie when they were children. They had followed their big brother around like anxious puppies, and he never failed to include them in his games or his chores, making them feel very grown-up. Evie drew her Milky War bar out and handed it to Jeannie, keeping Albert's safely stowed away for later.

"See if this helps."

Jeannie's eyes widened, and she glanced around the bus like Evie had offered her a stolen watch. "I can't accept this. Chocolate is rationed."

"It's okay. I got it from the PX—the post exchange at Bushnell. Since we're a military hospital, we have candy and other treats. Go ahead."

With a guilty smile of thanks, Jeannie took the bar and unwrapped the wax paper. She bit into the nougat and caramel and closed her eyes. "Mmm. Heavenly. I'd almost forgotten what chocolate tastes like. Oh!" She put her hand on her belly. "The baby likes it too!"

Evie laughed along with Jeannie, relieved to see color returning to the other woman's face. The bus crept around turns and made a couple of other stops on its way to the hospital.

"No!" cried a familiar, sour voice. "I won't ride on a bus with her!"

Evie worried for a moment that the woman was talking about her, but she craned her neck to see the sour-faced woman pointing to a girl in a nurse's uniform. A Japanese girl.

The sour woman shook her umbrella at the Japanese nurse.

"My poor Tommy is never coming home because of people like you!" She spat on the nurse's white uniform. "You don't deserve to ride this bus!"

The quiet murmur of the passengers turned deathly quiet. Evie and Jeannie shared a look of embarrassed discomfort.

The bus bumped over to the side of the road and the door hissed open.

"Get off," the driver commanded.

Evie sat taller, straining to see. The Japanese might kill Albert too, and there were posters all over town reminding people to be on the lookout for saboteurs and spies. Evie wasn't sure how she felt about a Japanese nurse, but throwing her off the bus on such a cold morning without proof she'd done anything wrong?

The driver wasn't talking to the nurse, though. His glare was fixed on the sour woman.

"You heard me. You're creating a disturbance. Get off my bus."

The woman and the driver stared at each other for so long, an unreal feeling drifted over the bus. Evie glanced at her watch. They were going to be late after all.

"Go on, go!" another man shouted from the back. "We have places to be."

The old woman grabbed her umbrella and marched off, yelling threats at the nurse and the driver the entire time.

Evie sat down and gripped the seat in front of her to still her shaking hands. The old woman had a right to be angry, didn't she? Her son was dead, part of her heart cut out by the war. But was it fair to assume that every Japanese person had something to do with the war? The government thought so, rounding up all the Japanese living on the West Coast and putting them in camps so they couldn't cause trouble. But there were Japanese-American patients at Bushnell who had fought for the US and lost limbs in the process, members of the highly-decorated 442nd regimental combat team. If there really were spies everywhere, Evie didn't know how to tell who she could trust.

The bus ride continued in perfect silence, except a muffled sob from the nurse. They turned off the road, passed the guards stationed by the front gate of the hospital, and swung past the flagpole to stop in front of the hospital administration building. The Japanese nurse was the first one off, and she hurried away without looking back.

"Come on," Evie said quietly to Jeannie. "I'll show you to someone who can help you find your husband."

They climbed down from the bus, and Jeannie gaped at the two-story tan brick buildings with military-green roofs, all lined up in front of them like soldiers waiting for review.

"It's so big!" Jeannie clutched her belly protectively.

"We've got almost 2,000 beds," Evie said with a smile. "Not to mention our own mess halls, bakeries, laundry, fire station, and laboratories."

"It's a city."

"It is, but they'll take good care of you. Come on."

Evie walked as quickly as she could, aware of the work waiting for her on her desk, but Jeannie could only move so fast. They entered the front doors of the administration building. After the rows of offices, long, white hallways stretched out, connecting the various ward buildings so a patient didn't have to go outside to get from one place to another. Handy in the snowy Utah winters.

Jeannie wrinkled her nose as they walked past doorways that opened into various hospital wards. Evie had gotten used to the hospital smells of bleached linens and iodine, but she supposed the pregnant woman had a more sensitive nose.

Evie glanced at the ticking clocks that they past, each one reminding her: *You're late, you're late, you're late.* But she couldn't leave Jeannie alone. They finally waddled their way down into the telephone exchange near the center of the Bushnell complex. A few soldiers in wheelchairs or on crutches chatted with the girls working the telephones, and others sat on the low sofas, waiting their turn to make a phone call. A man with a hooked prosthetic arm picked up a bottle of Coke, the hooks opening and closing like a pair of dull scissors in response to the movements of his opposite shoulder. All the men wore the dark blue slacks and button-up shirts of the hospital, stitched with USA MD on the left-hand side of their chest, a reminder that they were still US soldiers, not yet discharged from the army.

Jeannie stared at the scene with wide eyes, then looked down, to the side, anywhere but at the wounded men. Evie remembered how shocked she had been the first time she'd walked into the hospital and seen the cost of their fight for the world's freedom, afraid even to glance at the patients for fear of offending them and at the same time wanting to stare and see if it was as horrifically real as it appeared. She took Jeannie by the arm.

"Come, dear, it will all seem normal to you in no time."

"So many wounded men."

"We have almost two-thousand beds here, remember. All full, all the time. When one man goes home, another takes his place. This is war. It doesn't end on the battlefield." Her face softened. "These men are glad to be here. They are alive, and they'll return to a normal life. Just like your husband will."

Jeannie swallowed hard and nodded. Evie found a telephone girl that she recognized and waved her over.

"Sue Ann, this is Jeannie Harding. She needs help finding her husband, George."

Sue Ann smiled and took possession of Jeannie. "Of course, honey. You come with me and we'll look at the directory."

Evie watched her go off, feeling guilty for not seeing her all the way into George's arms. But Sue Ann had her, and Evie was late. She walked at a fast clip down another long, white hallway, its monotony only broken by windows and doorways decorated with garland and tinsel, and up a ramp to her ward, ready to be taken to task for her tardiness.

Chapter Two

MAJOR ROSENBACH—the doctor Evie worked for—paced in front of her empty office at the front of their ward. The dim light painted his silvering hair a dull gray, and his bushy eyebrows frizzed upwards, giving him a perpetually surprised look. Lately, his normal smile had been replaced by a worried frown. This morning it bordered on a scowl.

"You're late, Miss Lewis!"

"Sorry, sir! It won't happen again."

"I have some notes to dictate to you, and then Lieutenant Mead needs you to go with him and take shorthand while he examines the boys who need prosthetics."

"Yes, sir."

Evie swung into her seat and poised with her fingers over the typewriter keys, ready to redeem herself. Major Rosenbach made notes about patient statuses: healing amputation stumps, men progressing from wheelchairs to crutches, infections clearing up nicely with the use of the new "wonder drug," penicillin, first tested right there at Bushnell only the year before.

By the time Lieutenant Mead showed up for her, her fingertips were numb from typing. She was only too happy to follow the balding physical-therapist-turned-lieutenant past the offices and into the patient section of the ward. She spent less time there than in her office. The ward was a long, open room with white metal-framed beds running down each wall. Windows on each side let in the weak December sun, and a screened porch on the east held tables for ping pong and card games.

Many of the patients were in physical therapy sessions during the day, learning to walk again on prosthetic legs or practicing picking things up with their hooked hands, and in the workshops polishing job skills like radio repair or leatherworking for when they left the hospital. The ones left behind were those who weren't as mobile yet. They smoked and talked, English with a mix of Spanish and pidgin Hawaiian thrown in. Some tossed a ball around or read *Time* magazine.

When Lieutenant Mead finished his evaluations, he guided Evie out of the ward.

"It's like babysitting a room full of teenagers," Dr. Mead said as they regained the quiet of the hallway.

Evie forced a chuckle. The boys did seem young and ready to get into mischief, but every one of them—barely out of high school—had sacrificed body and mind for their country. It seemed too high a price to pay, but the thought of doing nothing and letting the fanatics in Germany and Japan spread their power across the globe was equally as impossible. At least every life saved at Bushnell and similar hospitals across the country was a small victory snatched from the Axis powers, and enough small victories would add up to the final triumph when the war was over and their boys could stop fighting and finally come home.

Lieutenant Mead dabbed his face with a handkerchief and then patted his balding head. "Doctor—I mean Major—Rosenbach said he could spare you a bit longer, so if you can take notes on one more ward for me, I'd appreciate it."

Evie nodded, and they walked down the hallway to the next ward. A gaudy profusion of tinsel, stringed lights, and pine garlands gathered on trips to the mountains hung around the doorway. The hospital was holding a contest for the best Christmas decorations, and each ward competed fiercely for the honor.

Evie and Lieutenant Mead passed a swarthy man mopping the floor, his tan shirt and pants splotched with a big, black "PW" to mark him as an enemy prisoner of war assigned to work in the hospital. He saluted Lieutenant Mead with mock seriousness, then grinned at Evie.

"Eh, bella donna!" he said in a heavy Italian accent. "I love you, pretty lady. You marry me?"

Evie flushed and ignored him, and Dr. Mead gave him a warning look. "No fraternization." He shook his head and turned an apologetic glance to Evie. "At least we're not over at the POW branch camp. A whole bunkhouse full of those guys would be enough to test anyone's patience."

"And their resolve to stay single," Evie added with a twinkle. The POWs were persistent in their efforts to flirt with the female employees of Bushnell. The foreign soldiers were treated well in hopes that American POWs overseas would be extended the same courtesy. Evie could only pray that it worked.

Dr. Mead laughed and gestured for her to go first into the next ward.

They finished up just in time for lunch, and Evie hurried back to her office. She opened her handbag and pulled out some stationary to write her weekly letter to her older brother.

December 4, 1944

Dear Albert,

I miss your letters. I hope you passed Thanksgiving in safety. We don't hear much about the war in India or China here, though I scan the papers every day.

I spent Thanksgiving here at Bushnell Hospital. It would have been nice to see Mom and Dad and Robbie, but it's not the same with the war on, and the boys in the hospital need cheering too. We ate a big dinner on the parade grounds and had a swell time. The last of the leaves have fallen, but we've only had a light dusting of snow in the mountains.

Evie paused, remembering past holiday sledding trips in the mountains with the whole family together, Albert pulling her and Robbie up the slopes while her parents cheered them on, and hot chocolate at the end of it when they'd tumbled into the snow a few times and their fingers were red and tingling from the cold.

"Are you coming to lunch, Evie?"

Evie blinked and looked up at her roommate, Fran, whose brown curls crowned her head in a poufy bouffant style. Evie glanced back at her letter and the work waiting on her desk. A blank sheet of white paper sat ready in the typewriter, and her notes were arranged in careful stacks, tapped until their edges lined up perfectly. The clock on the wall warned her she only had twenty minutes until lunch ended.

"I don't think I have time," Evie said apologetically. "Major Rosenbach had me take notes for Lieutenant Mead, and I still have to type them up."

Fran leaned against the doorframe and folded her arms. "You're always doing too much. The rest of us don't get extra work from our doctors."

"Major Rosenbach knows I'm efficient."

Fran leaned closer, keeping her voice down. "He knows he can get you to work too hard." She grabbed the Milky Way bar stashed in Evie's open handbag and waved it at her. "The slogan is, 'The sweet you can eat between meals,' not 'The sweet you can eat instead of meals.' You've got to take care of yourself."

Evie flushed. "The candy's not for me. They finally had it in the PX, so I got it for Albert. It's his favorite," she added quietly.

"Oh, sweetie." Fran placed the candy bar on the desk and gave Evie a quick hug. "You can't carry it all on your shoulders. I'll bring you back something from the mess hall."

"Thank you." Evie straightened the Milky Way so it lined up with the typewriter just so. "If it's not too much trouble."

Fran laughed. "Oh, you'll owe me big time. I'm not sure I can carry a sandwich soooo far."

Evie smiled, dimpling her cheeks. "Have a good lunch."

Fran waggled her fingers and walked off, joining another of the medical secretaries for the walk to the PX or the mess hall. The heels of their sensible shoes clacked away on the tile floor.

Evie turned back to the letter, but the spell had been broken. She folded the paper, lining it up so it divided into equal thirds, and slipped it into her handbag along with the Milky Way bar. Several other letters to Albert sat in the bottom of the bag, sealed in their envelopes but unaddressed except *2nd Lieutenant Albert Lewis, 341st Bombardment Group.*

"Miss Lewis?"

She jumped and found Major Rosenbach watching her from his adjoining office. The desk behind him was cluttered except a space cleared around a menorah patiently waiting for Hanukkah to begin.

"Yes, sir?"

He rubbed his bleary eyes, further frizzing his eyebrows. "I know it's still your lunch break, but they need those reports you typed up this morning over in the lab."

"Right away, sir!"

Evie gathered the reports and her handbag, not daring to leave it out on her desk with patients, therapists, nurses, cleaning staff, and heaven only knew who else wandering in and out of the ward during lunchtime. She hurried into the maze of hallways, trying to remember which turn to take to the lab. She reached the intersection of two long ramps and heard a whoop.

Something slammed into her leg and sent her wobbling off balance. The papers fluttered around her in a hailstorm of white. She looked up into a male face as surprised as her own.

"Excuse me," she muttered, not sure what had happened. How lucky this man had caught her.

The man's blue eyes sparkled. "Can I give you a ride somewhere?"

She looked down and saw that she was sitting in his lap, supported by his wheelchair. His friend, also in a wheelchair, grinned at them. They both wore the dark patient uniforms emblazoned with USA MD.

"You won this one, Glenn," his friend said with a laugh.

Evie swung to her feet. "Were you racing down the ramps? Didn't you think about how dangerous that is?"

"I think it turned out alright." Glenn's blue eyes sparkled with amusement.

Evie scooped up her papers, sorting them back into the right folders. "These are important!"

"Are you sure you don't want a ride? I'd offer you a hand"— he held up the hooked prosthesis in place of his left arm— "but I already gave one to the Italians."

His friend chortled again. Evie hesitated for a moment, impressed that a man with a prosthetic hook had been able to use a wheelchair at all, even if it was for a foolish race. Then she shook her head and stormed away. They were war heroes, but they still acted like children. She didn't understand it. And didn't they know that the research done at Bushnell could help improve their lives and save the lives of men still out in the field?

She arrived at the labs in a huff and handed over the folders to the bespectacled young technical sergeant in charge—Tech Sergeant Meyers. He looked through the stack and his forehead wrinkled.

"There's one missing."

"What? Are you sure? I had all of them together..." The crash. She must have dropped it. "I'll get it for you, sir. I'll be right back."

She hurried back down the labyrinth of corridors. Which one had that obnoxious man run her over in? Yes, turn there. That should have been it. But the corridors were empty, the floor swept clean. Had someone else picked it up? Or had she left it at her desk? She was sure she had it when she left. Pretty sure, anyway.

She quick-walked back up to the office. Her desk was still perfectly organized. No extra folders or any files out of place. In the wrong stack? She leafed through them quickly, but everything was where it should have been. She scurried back down to the lab, trying not to show that she was out of breath, and found Sergeant Meyers again.

"Yes?" he asked, pushing his glasses up on the bridge of his nose.

"The file..." she panted. How could she explain that she'd lost it?

"Your friend brought it by." He held it up.

"My friend?" she asked, but the technical sergeant gave her a nod and turned back to the row of microscopes on the counter, whistling.

Nurses in belted white dresses hovered over test tubes and compared notes. More tests on penicillin or malaria medications or some other new medical breakthrough. Evie felt a vicarious thrill seeing their work going forward. They were saving wounded soldiers—that was enough by itself—but while they did so, they were making discoveries that would help everyone.

A poster on the wall declared, *Penicillin Saves Soldiers Lives! Men who might have died will live if you give this job everything you've got!* Next to it was another that showed a curvy, seductive woman with a glass of wine and the warning, *Keep mum, she's not dumb!* The last depicted a wounded soldier and proclaimed, *Thanks to penicillin, he will come home!*

"I hope so," Evie whispered, walking on. She glanced in her purse and stumbled to a stop. Albert's Milky Way bar. It was gone too. She muttered a word that would get her in trouble with her mother. Or would have, if she hadn't learned it from her mother in the first place.

That soldier, Glenn. Had he picked up the file and Albert's Milky Way bar? It was nice enough of him to return the file, but he didn't deserve Albert's candy bar. Maybe the PX had more. Evie glanced at her watch and back at the poster on the wall.

Men who might have died will live if you give this job everything you've got.

She had to get back to work. She hoped Glenn choked on the candy.

She slid into her chair just as the lunch hour ended. As she did, she wondered briefly how Glenn had known where to take the file.

Chapter Three

FIVE O'CLOCK CAME around, and Evie leaned back in her chair to stretch. She glanced at the shorthand notes still waiting for transcription and sighed. Back to work.

A few minutes later, Fran poked her head in the door.

"Ready for dinner?"

"Well..."

"I'm not letting you skip another meal. If you pass out, I'll have to drag you back to our room."

Evie chuckled. "Okay, okay. I just need to stop by the PX. Some...jerk took Albert's Milky Way bar." She glanced at her friend. "I sound silly, don't I?"

"Oh, sweetie. We all have to do things to keep up hope."

Evie shrugged. Was it hope, this dull, heavy gnawing in her stomach?

They strolled down the ramps to the post exchange. In an age of rationing, it was like Aladdin's treasure cave. Candy, chocolate, milkshakes, and other things to make Evie's mouth water. But no Milky Way bars on the shelves. They had the dark version, Forever Yours, which Evie particularly liked, but Albert didn't care for them.

"You have time to keep checking," Fran said as they left. "After all, you don't even know—" She stopped and pretended to cough.

"We don't even know if he's alive," Evie finished quietly.

"But if they haven't found his plane, there's a chance he was forced down and captured."

Evie nodded dully. His plane could have gone down in the ocean, though, and then they would never know. And if the Japanese had captured him, well, she had heard rumors of the treatment of American POWs. They certainly weren't mopping hallways and flirting with girls.

Fran and Evie got their dinners in silence. Evie ate without really tasting anything. It was another thing to be grateful for, though, that she could eat at Bushnell and not be a drain on her parents' ration cards.

"Do you want to go to a movie?" Fran asked.

"I don't know. There's so much work to do, and I want to save my money. Maybe after Christmas."

Fran pursed her lips. "You said that about Thanksgiving, and then about your visit to your brother. You've got to have *fun* sometimes, Evie."

Evie ignored her friend, her eyes fastening on a familiar figure across the mess hall. Glenn. She could find out if he was the one who picked up the missing file and how he knew where to take it.

"Excuse me," she said to Fran and strode across the room.

Glenn was sitting with his wheelchair-racing friend, though this time both men had crutches leaning up against the table. So, they didn't even need wheelchairs—they'd just been horsing around. Glenn perked up when he saw Evie coming.

"I never thought I'd see you again. Couldn't stay away?" He took a bite of the Milky Way bar.

"That was Albert's!" She pointed at the candy.

He looked down at the half-eaten candy. "Who's Albert?"

"Never mind that. You took it from me!"

"I found it on the floor. Do you know how much work it was to reach down and get it without falling on my face?"

"I wish you *had* fallen on your face and wiped away that smug smirk!"

Glenn's friend laughed. "She has you there. You are a smug—" His friend hesitated and looked at Evie. "I mean, you have a smug—"

"Oh, go ahead and call him whatever you were going to say. He deserves it."

Now Glenn laughed. "Maybe I do. Do you want your candy back?"

Evie wrinkled her nose and the half-eaten bar. "Not now. I suppose you were so busy stealing it that you didn't see who picked up the file I dropped."

"File?"

"Yes, the missing file that made me look incompetent."

"I'm sure you're nothing of the sort."

Glenn sounded sincere, but Evie steamed at him. "Of course, I'm not. You're the one who crashed into me."

"And, surprisingly, I still can't bring myself to regret it," Glenn said with a grin. "But there was nothing on the ground but the candy bar. Trust me, I got a good look while trying not to crush my smug face."

"Oh, it's not like you would have noticed anyway."

Evie stormed away, her face burning. Why couldn't she keep her temper with that man? He just must not have seen the file. But that seemed unlikely. If she hadn't dropped it there, where could she have left it for someone else to pick it up? Maybe her worry over Albert was distracting her too much from doing the thing that would actually help him if—no, when—they did find him.

"Well, that's not my idea of fun," Fran said when Evie returned to the table, "but I'm glad to see you amusing yourself. He's handsome."

Evie blinked at her. "What? Who?"

"The soldier you were flirting with."

"That was not flirting!"

"I didn't say it was *good* flirting, but you've obviously got his attention. He watched you all the way back over here."

Evie rolled her eyes. "I'm sure he thinks I'm a lunatic." Evie quickly told her friend about the crash in the hallway and the missing file.

Fran frowned. "I don't know. You must have left it on your desk, and Major Rosenbach sent someone else over with it."

Evie stabbed at the remnants of the chicken and green beans on her plate. "Yes, I suppose so."

"Sweetie, even you are allowed to forget things sometimes. I'm telling you, you need that break at the movies."

Evie sat back and stared at the ceiling. Maybe she did need a change. If she worked too hard, she might lose her ability to focus. "Oh, fine."

"Let's go tonight, then!" Fran pulled out a copy of the *Bugle*, the hospital newspaper. "They're showing *Lifeboat* again—that one where the sub attack survivors rescue a sailor from the U-Boat that sank them."

Evie mulled it over. "Isn't that a Hitchcock film?"

"Yeah."

"No, I want something funny. Something *not* about the war."

"Then it looks like we'll be seeing *Meet Me in St. Louis*."

The girls left the mess hall and walked through the covered hallways for the short outside trip to the hospital theater. They weren't the only ones catching a Monday night movie, but most of the boys from the hospital were lining up for *Lifeboat*.

"I don't understand why they want to watch movies about the war," Evie said once she and Fran were settled in their seats. "I would think they'd want nothing more to do with it."

"Maybe it provides some kind of comfort. Helps them remember why they did it, or that it's not just all a bad dream."

Sergeant Meyers took a seat a few rows ahead of them with a platinum blonde girl. They whispered to each other, the blonde giggling while the tech sergeant adjusted his glasses and grinned at her. Evie rolled her eyes. Maybe they should have gone to see *Lifeboat* after all. She didn't want to sit through a date movie.

The newsreel started its unrelenting images of battle: Allied troops marching past bombed-out medieval buildings in Metz,

France, Japanese *kamikaze* pilots smashing their planes into the USS *Intrepid*, and the Japanese troops pushing deeper into China. Evie leaned forward, squinting to see more, deeper, into those clips of blurry faces, hoping, somehow, to catch a glimpse of Albert. He was out there, somewhere. Someone knew where he was, even if it was just the Japanese pilot who had shot him down. But no. She couldn't think like that, even though the long absence of letters from him, or any sign of his plane, made it the most likely reality, looking more like a certainty every day.

Evie almost sighed in relief when the opening credits started for *Meet Me in St. Louis*. But the bright songs jarred her, Judy Garland's smile struck her as false, and she couldn't bring herself to laugh or tap her foot along as Fran did. She was almost as glad when the movie ended as she had been when it started.

"See, wasn't that fun?" Fran asked, linking arms with her to stroll outside.

Evie nodded absently as Fran hummed "Have Yourself a Merry Little Christmas" from the movie.

"Miss Lewis?" Someone tugged gently on her sleeve.

Evie turned to find Jeannie grinning up at her, her hand on the arm of a young soldier with a bright, round face and a pair of crutches.

"Jeannie! This must be your George." She pulled Fran to a stop. "Fran, this is Jeannie and her husband George Harding. She's here awaiting the stork's arrival."

Jeannie smiled shyly. "I told George how kind you were to me. I thought I'd never see you again, this place is so big."

"It is," Evie said, "but it's small too. I'm glad to see you settled in."

"Thank you for watching out for her," George said. "We're from a little place in Washington, and before the war, neither of us had gone any farther than Spokane. This has all been quite an adventure."

"I bet you'll be glad when it's over," Evie said. "You get to return home a hero."

George stiffened, and some of the light went out of his face. "Oh, no, miss. I'm not *combat wounded*, you see. I was *injured* in a training accident."

Evie wrinkled her forehead in confusion. "But you were still serving your country."

George gave her a sad little smile and shook his head in a way that reminded Evie that she was an outsider to what these boys had been through, and she couldn't really understand their world.

"Well, I'm just happy we're here together now." Jeannie's eyes shone when she looked at her husband.

Evie smiled. She was glad George was so far along in his recovery: already walking on crutches. It had to make it less overwhelming for Jeannie, especially with a baby coming. And the way George looked at Jeannie, like he'd been a starving man and she'd brought him a feast.

"Best of luck," Evie said. "I'll look forward to seeing the baby announcement in the *Bugle*."

She and Fran headed off toward their room near the nurses' quarters. Fran chatted happily about the movie, but Evie remained uncomfortably aware of a sense that something was missing. The war was too real, the movies were too fake, and that warm contentment shining from Jeannie and George was too elusive.

Chapter Four

THE REST OF THE week passed by in a flurry of note-taking and clacking typewriter keys. Evie relished the busy schedule. Each day brought her closer to...something. An end to the war? An answer about Albert? Regardless, it was progress. Movement forward, evidenced by the stacks of paper that grew and went to be replaced by more. Neat, clean information. All the chaos, confusion, and uncertainty of war contained on crisp, white sheets of paper. She dreaded the quiet of the weekend when it came around and mumbled her way through the Christmas carols at church. She wasn't in the mood for it this year. Next year would be better.

Monday morning, Evie arrived early. She'd had nightmares about Albert's plane floating in the ocean, just scattered, lifeless wreckage of metal, the water stained red with oil and blood. She had to get the image out of her head. Maybe if she started early, she could leave a bit early too and catch up on sleep before the weekend.

"Pretty lady!" The Italian POW paused from cleaning the glass and opened a door for her. "You come back to marry me?"

She shook her head, trying not to laugh at his mock-hurt expression as she passed by. They weren't even allowed to talk to the POWs to avoid anyone getting romantically entangled with the enemy or passing on sensitive information.

Evie settled back at her desk for another day of work. But one of her stacks was off center. She frowned and straightened it. Maybe someone had moved it when they cleaned her desk. But the corner of one of the file folders stuck out at an odd angle. She tried to push it back in, but the folders on top were too heavy. She could only tug it loose by pushing against the rest of the stack and giving it a good yank.

She stared at the folder. The piles were all neat when she'd left on Friday night. This hadn't happened by accident. Someone had pulled the file out, and they'd tried to shove it back in so she wouldn't know. If her desk were as messy as Major Rosenbach's, she might never have noticed. She glanced out at the poster in the hallway, the one that showed a soldier falling under enemy fire and said, *Careless talk costs lives.*

Evie didn't blab about her job, but she'd never seriously considered that she knew anything important. The men at Bushnell were done with the fighting. Any information they had about conditions on the fronts was months out of date. Yet, someone had been going through her files. A nurse who needed more information on a patient? But why not just ask? Could someone have a grudge or concerns about one of the men, trying to ferret out details about them? Evie opened the folder to see what it contained.

It was notes on a patient named Corporal Gary Higa. He'd been shot through the spinal cord and arrived at Bushnell with an infection in his lungs, but it had cleared up with penicillin. His prognosis was fair: he wasn't expected to walk again but otherwise was recovering well.

Why the interest in Corporal Higa? Spinal cord injury survivors were relatively uncommon, even at Bushnell, but that information didn't seem exceptional. Was it because he was Japanese American, part of the famed 442nd division?

Major Rosenbach walked into his office and dropped his coat on the back of his chair before settling at his desk. Evie rose and took the report to show him.

"Sir, I have a concern."

"Oh, what is it Miss Lewis?" His eyebrows crawled up and down in annoyance at her interruption. But what if the report mattered somehow?

"I believe someone was going through the papers on my desk. Particularly this file."

His brow wrinkled, and he studied the papers. "Ah, Corporal Higa. What makes you think someone looked at it?"

"It was out of place—not neatly stacked, but like someone had shoved it back in the pile."

Major Rosenbach glanced at the leaning stacks of folders on his desk and over at Evie's neat workspace. He grunted. "Maybe they just knocked it over and straightened it back up in a hurry. None of this information is classified."

"Yes, sir."

He handed the report back and dismissed her with a glance.

Evie wandered back to her desk and placed the folder back in its place in the pile. It didn't look like anything else on her desk had been disturbed. She had done her duty and reported her suspicion. Yet, it nagged at her. This was the second time in a week something odd had happened with her files. What if the missing file from the lab reports hadn't been there when she crashed in the hallway? What if it had been missing before she'd picked them up for the dash down the hall, and the person who took it had simply delivered it where it should have gone, or left it for someone else to deliver? And what kind of files went to the lab? Reports on patients and infections.

Evie glanced at the clock. It would be easy enough to ask more next time she went to the lab, and when she had these reports typed up, that was where some of them would go. She got to work, attempting to break her speed-typing record as she entered all her shorthand from Major Rosenbach and Lieutenant Mead's reports. Before lunch time, she had a fresh armful of files to take down to the lab.

She walked carefully, making sure she wouldn't have another accident in the hallways. It was quieter this time since the men hadn't stampeded to the mess hall yet. A muted whistle from outside announced the arrival of another train bringing medical supplies or new patients to Bushnell, but an almost-reverent stillness gripped the lab. The technicians huddled around microscopes and test tubes, finding answers where Evie only saw riddles.

Evie passed off the papers to the same technician she had dealt with before—Sergeant Meyers. He took them with hardly more than a nod and returned to his work.

"Excuse me," Evie said.

He turned back and squinted at her through his glasses. "Yes?"

"I wondered if you remembered last week when the folder was missing?"

He looked confused for a moment. "Oh, right. Yes?"

"Who was it that delivered it?"

A look flashed in his eyes. Alarm? Then, he shrugged. "I don't recall."

"Do you remember anything—"

"We got the folder. It's in the past. I need to get back to work."

Evie stared after him. What was that about? He was clearly lying to her. But why? He had access to all the information in the lab, so why would he need to sneak looks at copies of it?

Evie wandered blindly out of the lab. Based on the noise in the halls, the rush for the mess hall had begun. She should get some lunch too. Fran would be looking for her. Everyone said the mystery of the folders wasn't important. And yet, and yet, and yet...

The poster on the wall still proclaimed, *Men who might have died will live if you give this job everything you've got.*

"This has nothing to do with Albert," she whispered back to the poster. "I can't help him."

But the tech sergeant was lying, and someone was snooping around in her files.

Maybe while they were all supposed to be eating.

Evie hurried through the warren of hallways and ramps, slowing her steps and trying to keep her fast breathing quiet as she neared her ward. Someone was humming. She peeked around the corner. The Italian POW polished the windows in the offices, humming a Christmas tune to himself, slightly out of key.

The Italian had the opportunity to steal information from the files, and perhaps a motive as well if he hated the United States. Evie shrank back, watching without being seen. The POW finished the window and started to turn in her direction. She ducked back behind the door, listening. The Italian made plenty of noise as he sang "White Christmas" badly and thumped around, dusting or mopping. Evie couldn't tell if he was at her desk. She could surprise him by walking in the room, but would it be better if he didn't know she was on to him? His humming stopped, and the room grew quiet. She had to know what he was doing.

Evie stepped into the doorway and had just a moment to catch the Italian. He had paused in emptying her wastebasket and was staring wistfully out the window, past the brown lawns and rows of green-roofed hospital buildings toward the wild, snow-dusted mountaintops. He signed heavily and finished emptying the wastebasket. She backed out into the hallway, picking some silver tinsel out of her dark blonde hair.

She hadn't learned anything. The Italian could be a spy, but she would have to catch him in the act. And she couldn't be blind to the possibility that there might be someone else. Even if the POW was taking information—and that was assuming his English was good enough to make sense of the technical reports—he had to be working with someone else. The POWs who were cleared to work in the hospital could wander its halls, but they weren't supposed to leave the base. Unless he had a girl somewhere who fell for his, "Pretty lady, please marry me." And would that girl help spy on her own country for those dark Italian eyes? Evie would like to think not, but she knew girls who had done dumber things.

She would have to watch the Italian, but she couldn't ignore the fact that Sergeant Meyers was hiding something as well, and she didn't know who else might be sneaking around. That meant she was going to have to do some sneaking as well.

Chapter Five

AFTER LUNCH, MAJOR Rosenbach called Evie to his office. The first candle had appeared in his menorah, but otherwise his desk was as disordered as ever.

"Lieutenant Mead needs some extra assistance with the new patients. You've done a good job of keeping up with your notes, so I'd like you to help him again—not just with shorthand, but working with the patients a little as well."

Evie shifted feet. "But, I'm not a nurse."

"We're short of nurses, and Lieutenant Mead was impressed with your bedside manners last time."

"Yes, sir." It was more work and more time away from her desk, but this would give her a chance to find out if anything suspicious was going on in the ward.

Lieutenant Mead was waiting for Evie, his bald head a bright reflection of the overhead lights. She cast an anxious glance at the files on her desk then followed him through the Christmas garlands and into the ward.

"We have a lot of new patients who aren't mobile yet," Mead said, glancing back as she scurried behind him. "I'll need to assess their conditions, and I could use someone who can talk to them. Make them feel assured. Your face is friendlier than mine, and you're a no-nonsense girl, so you won't get offended if they're rude."

"I understand, sir."

But when they walked into the ward, Evie hesitated at the somber stillness. Most of the beds were empty, as the boys in wheelchairs and prosthetics were out doing therapy, but several held new patients who weren't even sitting up yet. Unlike the boisterous soldiers who were nearly recovered, these men were almost deathly quiet, except one who moaned occasionally.

Lieutenant Mead approached that young man, Private Smith, first and examined the stump of his missing leg. Private Smith barely acknowledged their presence.

Lieutenant Mead drew Evie aside. "They'll need to re-amputate his stump. It's a battlefield surgery and has become infected," he said in a low voice as she took notes in shorthand. "They should have treated it before, but the nurses tell me they came up short on penicillin from the most recent shipment." He hesitated and glanced out toward the hall. "Can you keep Private Smith company for a moment?"

"Of course." Evie sat in a chair by Private Smith's bed while Lieutenant Mead stepped outside the ward. Maybe sneaking off for a cigarette break, though Evie had never noticed him smelling of smoke. The only smell she noticed now was the faint stink of infection from the soldier's wound, but they would clean that up as soon as the trains brought more penicillin. She smiled at the young private.

"I'm Evelyn Lewis. Since I'm not in the army, maybe I can call you by your first name?"

The young man rolled his head to the side to give her a critical stare, then turned away.

"Lieutenant Mead is an excellent therapist. He'll have you walking again in no time, and then you'll be on your way home."

Nothing.

She plastered on a smile. "Where did you serve?"

A slow blink. Then nothing.

Evie shifted uncomfortably. So far, she was batting zero in her new role. Some boys didn't like to talk about their service, so she tried a different tactic.

"Well, I'll tell you a bit about Bushnell and Brigham City, then. You probably came in by train, and I guess they had the windows covered? Wait until you can get a good look outside. The mountains are stunning. And we might have a white Christmas. That's nice to look forward to."

Christmas could be a sensitive topic, though, since it made some of the boys homesick.

"Helen Keller is coming to visit this week. She's blind and deaf, and I hear she's very inspirational. I bet we'll have you in a wheelchair in time to go see her, and she may visit the wards as well. A lot of our boys here does sports. You can play volleyball sitting on the floor, or wheelchair basketball, until you get on your feet. And there's a theater."

Lieutenant Mead came back to hover beside Evie. Her face warmed a little under his watchful eye. She must have said everything wrong, because the young soldier still wouldn't look at her.

"We'll see you tomorrow, private," Lieutenant Mead said and guided Evie to another patient.

The next couple of young men were more attentive, listening as Lieutenant Mead outlined their recovery and asking nervous questions, sometimes in a whisper so Evie wouldn't hear. They had to be used to a lack of privacy in the military, but they weren't used to being watched by a woman not in a nurse's uniform. Their eyes looked haunted, like the soldiers were trying to put on a brave face while fear still lurked behind them. Evie glanced around, half-afraid she would see the same battle ghosts that darkened their expressions. She chatted where she could and smiled to put them at ease, and a few of them rewarded her with huge grins when all she did was call them by name. It humbled her to be able to temporarily dispel their gloom, and by something so simple.

Some of the more mobile patients trickled back in from their therapy sessions in the gym, including a familiar face: Glenn of the bright blue eyes.

"Are you ready to try on your new prosthetic leg, Private Holbrook?" Lieutenant Mead asked him. "I think we have the adjustments right this time."

Glenn glanced at Evie, looking a little nervous. "Oh, I suppose," he said with casual bravado.

"Don't worry. Miss Lewis is just here to assist me."

Glenn smiled. "Miss Lewis, is it? Good to finally know your name."

"Down to business," Lieutenant Mead said. He had Glenn sit and strap on his prosthetic leg while Evie took notes on the fit.

"Now, stand up."

Glenn did, getting shakily to his feet. He exhaled sharply and laughed. "I'm standing!"

His grin was contagious, and Evie smiled back.

He wiped his eyes. "When that grenade went off, I didn't know if I'd even live. My leg...it was just gone. I never thought I'd stand again."

"The miracle of modern medicine," Lieutenant Mead said. "Excuse me."

He left Evie and Glenn alone for a moment.

"Help me," Glenn said. "I want to walk."

"Maybe you should wait."

He laughed. "I've waited long enough. What could go wrong?"

Evie raised an eyebrow. "Well, you could fall, damage your stump, have to have another amputation, and then need to wait until it heals so they can fit you with another new prosthesis."

Glenn chuckled. "You're good at this game. Here I go."

He took a step forward, and Evie scrambled to reach out a hand and balance him.

"Are you crazy?" Evie asked.

"Maybe a little." Glenn lowered his voice, "But don't tell the doc or they'll lock me up in the NP Ward. I like it better here. They have basketball and no bars on the windows."

Evie chuckled in spite of herself. "Okay, Mister Wise Guy, sit back down until Lieutenant Mead gets back. I don't want you to fall and crack your head open."

"You'd hate to see me ruin my smug face?"

"No, my shoes." Evie grinned. "With rationing on, these have to last me *years*. Plus, I don't want to get fired. You've already gotten me in trouble once."

Glenn sat and rubbed at his leg above the prosthetic limb. "Did you really get in trouble?"

"Only a little." Evie hesitated. "When you crashed into me—"

"*You* crashed into *me*."

"Ha!" She rolled her eyes. "But after that, did you see anyone else in the hallway?"

Glenn looked thoughtful. "I suppose a couple of people."

"Do you remember who?"

"Not really. No one who stood out. Maybe a nurse or a couple of patients. Why?"

"One of my files was missing. It turned up later, but... well, it was odd that it disappeared."

He shrugged. "Sorry I can't be more help."

Lieutenant Mead returned. "What are you doing sitting? Come on, back up."

Evie winced inwardly since it had been her idea that Glenn should sit. She took notes as he practiced with his prosthetic leg. The brace shop really did work wonders. Parts of the prosthetics were plastic, making them lighter and less likely to cause blisters. It was good work they were doing at Bushnell, and Evie was a part of it. When the war was over, she'd be able to look back and be proud that she helped.

Lieutenant Mead glanced at his watch. "Keep practicing with the prosthetic."

He led Evie to a bed-bound patient with Asian features.

"Corporal Higa, how are you feeling today?"

Evie's attention jerked to the corporal. So, this was the man whose file had been rifled through. But why? She studied him as Lieutenant Mead continued his examination.

Corporal Higa shrugged. "I'm pretty good from the waist up. Otherwise, no change."

Evie took in the young man's condition. The outline of his legs showed through the sheets, but they didn't move naturally as he struggled to sit up. Some soldiers with spinal cord damage could still move a little below the injury, but not Corporal Higa.

Lieutenant Mead nodded. "At this point, I think it's fair to say nothing is going to change. You'll need to learn to work with what you have."

Evie glanced in surprise at Lieutenant Mead's matter-of-fact tone, but Corporal Higa didn't flinch from it. He considering the doctor with thoughtful eyes.

"Any chance of me being able to walk with braces of some kind?"

"Possibly for short distances, but you should focus on becoming adept with a wheelchair. And with that upper body strength, you'll be able move yourself in and out of bed, onto chairs, and around your job. Your grip strength is fine, so you can do most manual tasks."

"Yes, sir. I've been taking classes on radio repair, and I like it."

Evie took down Lieutenant Mead's thoughts on Corporal Higa's progress, and they made their exit from the ward.

Lieutenant Mead let out a long sigh. "It's amazing how the days go by so fast yet feel so long."

Evie nodded. The work day was almost over. "I should get these typed up."

She stayed late to type up all the reports and gave the stacks of papers waiting on her desk a baleful glance. Setting them into neat piles, she pulled out a fresh sheet of stationary.

Dear Albert,

I stared today into the eyes of war, and it is a fearful thing that threatens to swallow me if I look too long. How can mankind do this to itself? To each other? All around me, Christmas lights flash, and I wonder that more of the boys aren't in the neuro-psychological ward, remembering the flashes on the battlefield. I have only seen the echoes of them, and I jump each time I hear a door bang.

What has this war done to you? You were always there for me and Robbie to pick us up and defend us against the bugbears of our imaginations. And now you're out there defending us against things so terrible I could never have imagined them.

What can I do that will ever be enough to repay you? If you have not already given your life, are you sacrificing your health or your sanity?

I pray daily that God, at least, sees where you are and is watching over you. I always wished that I could give some of my health to Robbie, and now I would give all of it to you, to have you safe and whole and home with us again.

All my love,
Evie

Chapter Six

As soon as Evie walked in to the office the next morning, her glance caught on her desk. Files were scattered across her workspace and over the chair and floor.

"No, no, no!"

She stooped to pick up an armful of folders, trying to sort which notes went to which file.

Major Rosenbach cleared his throat behind her.

"Sir!" Evie jumped to attention, a few stray papers drifting to the ground like white flags.

He looked over her shoulder at the mess. "I'm concerned about you. You've been a hard worker, but the state of your office is unacceptable."

"I know, sir."

"You know?"

"It wasn't like that when I left last night."

"Well, take care that in the future you don't stack your files so high." He hesitated and studied her face. "This isn't like you. Should I tell Lieutenant Mead to find someone else to help him?"

"No, you don't have to." That was her chance to find out more about Corporal Higa and whomever was sabotaging her work.

"Don't let yourself get behind."

"Yes, sir."

Evie's files had not been stacked too high. Someone had come through after she had left and sorted through them, not even bothering to hide it this time. Why? Did they get caught in the act? Or were they trying to get her fired?

It would be easy enough for someone to access to her desk after normal working hours. Bushnell was a hospital, and there was a night shift of guards, doctors, and nurses. Maybe janitors too. But not the POWs. They had strict rules about when they could work, and guards escorted them back to their barracks each evening.

Evie leaned her head against the bare white wall. If it wasn't the Italian POW, then who had been at her desk in the middle of the night?

Lieutenant Mead strolled into the ward, yawning blearily. Evie cleaned up as quickly as she could and caught up with him. He rubbed the top of his bald scalp and stifled another yawn.

"Late night?" Evie asked.

"There's always more paperwork to catch up on."

Paperwork. Evie kept her gaze forward, but she longed to study his face for signs of guilt. Could the therapist want something with her files? Maybe he had made a mistake somewhere, and he was trying to cover it up. He did seem twitchy sometimes. Yet, Evie hadn't heard of any problems with his patients. They were making good progress.

Still, she kept a sharp eye on all of them as they made their rounds. Private Smith was missing that day, having gone in for surgery. As the ambulatory patients marched by on their way to morning exercises, Glenn paused and handed her something. A candy bar.

Evie took it, her cheeks warming. It was a Forever Yours bar—the Milky Way with dark chocolate.

"I figured I owed you," Glenn said.

Evie's first instinct was to shove it back at him. He didn't understand. This wasn't Albert's favorite. But Glenn was trying to be nice. At least, she thought he was.

"Thank you," she muttered.

When she got back to her desk, she stuffed the candy bar in her purse. She'd save it for another time.

Private Smith was back the next day, his freshly re-amputated leg wrapped in white bandages. Lieutenant Mead stopped to greet him while a nurse checked the bandages and sprinkled some penicillin powder on his sutures.

Lieutenant Mead then brushed past Evie and out into the hallway. Evie watched the therapist with a frown. This wasn't the first time he had left Private Smith.

She sat next to the young soldier, hoping to learn more about him.

"It's a lovely day outside," she said. "It won't be long before you're able to go out and enjoy it. We may have snow soon. Do you like the snow?"

The private made no response. She continued her mindless, upbeat chatter to no avail, and she almost breathed a sigh of relief when Lieutenant Mead returned and cut her off.

"Well, private," Mead said, "it looks like your surgery was a success. Once your stump is healed, we can start making your prosthesis."

The young man didn't respond, just turned his head to face the wall. Evie watched him with concern. He was recovering, so what kept him in such low spirits?

Corporal Higa was quite the opposite. He laughed and joked with Lieutenant Mead and showed off the progress he'd made with his calisthenics and other exercises.

"You sure you can't get me some artificial legs too, Doc?"

Lieutenant Mead smiled sadly. "I'm afraid it wouldn't do you any good. We could practice on the parallel bars in the gym to build your upper body strength. It's not quite the same as walking, but you'd be out of your chair and moving under your own power. You'll have to get stronger first, though."

"You got a deal." Higa looked down at his lifeless legs. "You know, I always thought I'd take more time to do some hiking once I was done with the army." He gestured toward the mountains out the window. "I guess I missed my shot." He grinned. "Too bad the Nazis didn't do the same."

Evie looked to Lieutenant Mead, not sure how to respond. But the Lieutenant looked pale and distracted as he flipped through his notes.

Higa gave Evie a rueful smile.

"Sorry if I make you uneasy. Talking to girls was another thing I thought I'd have a chance to practice after the war. Well, I've got all the time in the world for it now, but none of them will want to talk to me."

"Oh, that's not true!" Evie said. "You're a handsome young man. And a war hero."

"Ha! I didn't do anything heroic, but it's nice of you to say it."

He motioned her closer, and she sat in the chair next to his bed.

He lit a cigarette but just watched the tip glow. "I've been here longer than most of these other fellows, so I sort of feel a brotherly concern for them."

Evie nodded, not sure where he was going.

"It's good of you to try talking to Private Smith, even if he acts like he doesn't like it."

"I wish I could do more for him."

"You can." Higa ground out the cigarette and held it up. "Do you know what a luxury this is—the ability to waste? In France, I would have smoked it down to the last centimeter or traded it for something useful like a mouthful of Spam. Now, I light them and put them out just because I can."

"Okay?" Evie asked, confused.

"Look, Private Smith is still getting used to this. Try to imagine losing one of your limbs. You're lucky to be alive, but you feel like you've lost everything. Maybe you even feel like you should be in a coffin instead of a hospital bed.

Evie squeezed her eyes shut for a moment, trying to banish thoughts of her little brother Robbie when he had been so sick with polio and learned his leg would never be right again. "I think I understand," she whispered.

"You need time to grieve over it. We all do it in different ways, like with dark jokes or acting tough, but I've watched a lot of boys come and go, and I can promise you every one of them has cried at some point. Most don't want to do it in front of each other—and especially not in front of a young lady—but they need time to mourn. A time for everything, like it says in the Bible. Sometimes, it doesn't help to think about the past or the future. We just have to deal with right now."

"I see." Evie stole a glance at Smith's huddled form. "Thank you."

"Thanks for pretending to flirt with me. It really does make me feel better."

"I'm not," Evie said.

"Ah, don't feel bad. I know they tell the girls to do it, and I know you local girls would probably get the stink eye from everyone if you went on a date with a Japanese fellow anyway. But we're all secretly scared that no girl will ever talk to us again."

Evie flushed. She had started to forget that Higa was Japanese—he had become just one of the patients to her. "I meant I wasn't trying to flirt. I enjoy talking to you, and I want to help."

Higa smiled and lit the cigarette again, painting the air with the tendril of smoke. Lieutenant Mead called Evie away. She glanced around for Glenn, but he was out doing therapy somewhere. She wasn't sure why she cared, but she wondered how his prosthetic leg was working out for him.

Back at her desk, she carefully went again through the folders that had been dumped on the floor. Yes, there in the stack was Private Smith's folder. She had no way of knowing, though, if it was his notes the culprit had been interested in. Corporal Higa's notes were in a different pile, undisturbed. What was going on? She spent her lunch break looking through all of them, trying to find a common thread. But the person who had rifled through her files might have only been looking for one, and she couldn't be sure which.

She sighed and stacked the papers neatly again then returned to typing. At least if she was caught up on her work, she left less for anyone to look through.

When she stepped out of the front of the hospital building that evening, the POWs were just leaving for the day too. She spotted her Italian Romeo among the others. He perked up when he saw her and waved.

"Hey, pretty lady!"

The guard ordered him to be quiet. Evie shook her head and ignored him. As the men loaded into the back of the truck for the short ride to their camp south of the hospital, Evie risked a glance back. The Italian was watching her with a thoughtful gaze—not silly or flirtatious. She shivered. He might not have been the one who was going through her desk, but could he be working with someone? They were warned to watch out for spies, but if there really were spies about, how could she know who to trust?

Chapter Seven

"YOU HAVE TO go dancing, Evie. It's your patriotic duty. And this is part of the routine." Fran held up her eyebrow pencil.

Evie sighed and turned around. "This is the silliest thing I've done for the war effort."

Fran laughed and drew a line up the back of Evie's legs in imitation of a stocking seam. "Just don't cross your legs, or you'll ruin the effect."

"Isn't it more patriotic to show that I've given up my stockings? All those boys who parachuted into France will probably appreciate the sacrifice of that little bit of silk."

"I think they appreciate the effort of us pretending that everything's normal."

"Do you think so?" Evie twisted her legs around so she could inspect Fran's makeup job. "I talked to one of the patients today, and what he said made me think maybe we shouldn't be pretending so much."

Fran sat, patting down her freshly-tamed brown curls. "I suppose it depends on the soldier. Some of them don't mind talking about it, but a lot of them just want to forget it all and have a good time."

"Yes, I suppose we can worry about the war later."

"Exactly. We'll just have fun tonight."

But on the walk over to the Red Cross auditorium where the dances were held, Evie was sure that night wasn't going to be fun. It was all about duty. Keeping the boys' spirits up. It had nothing to do with her.

The auditorium was cleared of chairs, except around the edges, and decorated with red, white, and blue bunting. A live band blasted the rolling rhythms of swing from the stage, the trumpets screaming their high notes while the drums pounded out the beat. The patients had traded in their dark hospital clothes for the crisp neatness of their uniforms, and the nurses and college girls from nearby cities wore colorful dresses in floral or gingham patterns, their practical shoes traded for heels.

Evie and Fran circulated through the room, drinking Cokes and talking to patients. A patient asked Fran to dance, and Evie settled down in a chair to chat about home with a couple of boys still in wheelchairs. They laughed nervously and acted like she was as fascinating as a movie star. She remembered what Corporal Higa had said about being afraid to talk to girls and tried to act as down-to-earth as possible, almost like she was talking to Albert, if he were lucky enough to be in an Allied hospital somewhere.

Fran joined them again for a while until another patient approached her.

"I bet I can jitterbug with you, Miss Young," he said. He lifted his pant leg to show off a prosthetic leg. "Even with this."

Fran raised an eyebrow. "Well, that's ambitious of you. Let's see." She took his hand, and they rushed to the floor. The other patients turned their attention to their friend, who was swirling Fran around the floor in a flourish of polka dot skirts.

A tall man loomed next to Evie then leaned down. "I can't do any fancy moves, but would you care to dance with me?"

Evie looked up, prepared to say yes, and saw Glenn smiling nervously at her. She flushed a little and nodded.

The band switched tempos while Glenn and Evie found a place on the floor, and they began playing "Time Waits for No One" from *Shine On, Harvest Moon*. The saxophone sang a low, sultry melody. Glenn cleared his throat and placed his hook hand on Evie's waist, not meeting her eyes. They fell into the slow rhythm of the song, and the strangeness of the feel of the metal through her dress quickly vanished.

"You've been practicing," she said.

"Me? Oh, sure, I tango up and down the ward with the other boys after calisthenics each morning."

Evie chuckled. "Just being on your feet."

"Well, I was thinking about Helen Keller coming to visit this weekend. If she can do all the amazing things she does, I can walk again. I want to be able to give her a standing ovation when she comes."

"I don't think you'll have any trouble with that."

He wiggled the hook hand. "Well, I'm not much for clapping."

Evie blushed. "Oh, I didn't mean to tease you."

"It's alright." Glenn grinned. "Go ahead and tease me, as long as Albert won't mind."

"Albert?" Evie asked. "He's a little protective, but I don't think he'll care." And a sob choked in her throat. Right there, in the mind of the dance. She pulled back and wiped a tear.

"What's wrong?" Glenn asked, wrapping his good arm around her and guiding her away from the curious stares of the other dancers. "Are you alright?"

She nodded, but tears continued to slide down her face.

"This is stupid," Glenn said. "Obviously you're not alright. Come here. Tell me about it."

They sat at an out-of-the-way table.

"You have enough troubles," Evie said. "You don't need to hear mine. I'm supposed to be cheering you up."

"Being able to help—even just to listen—would cheer me up," Glenn said. "Sometimes, it's easier to hear about other people's problems."

Evie nodded and choked on another sob. "I don't know if Albert is ever coming home. He's—" she hiccupped. "He's gone missing. No sign of his plane. No word from him. Maybe the Japanese captured him. But maybe..."

She couldn't say it. She could not think of Albert lost in the cold ocean somewhere, shot down by an enemy plane.

Glenn put a warm arm around her, and she cried into his uniform.

"It's too terrible," she said. "War is too terrible. All of this." The music was too loud, too bright for the darkness of her fears.

"Yeah, it is."

Something in the simple truth of his words helped calm Evie. She dried her eyes and laughed ruefully. "Well, I'm in no position to cheer anyone up now. I think I have to call this night a bust."

"But do *you* feel better?" Glenn asked.

Evie shrugged. Did she? Maybe the hard tangle of fear in her chest was a little lighter.

A figure on the other side of the room caught her eye. That dark hair, and those teasing eyes. The Italian POW! But he was wearing an American uniform. Evie pointed. "I know him!"

The Italian ducked out of sight. Glenn stood unsteadily as Evie lowered her accusing finger.

"You know who?" he asked. "There are lots of familiar patients here."

"He's not a patient. He's a POW."

Glenn scanned the room. "You saw him here?"

"I..." Was she sure? He was hard to mistake, but her eyes were still puffy and sore from crying. "I'm pretty sure. But that can't be. They're under guard."

"Lots of strange things are possible," Glenn said. "But maybe you've had enough excitement for one night."

"Yes. I'll find Fran and see if she's ready to get going." She looked at him shyly. "Thank you."

He smiled, but it looked a little strained. "Any time."

Evie watched for the POW on the walk back to her quarters but saw nothing except the guards making their rounds. Back in her room, before she could sleep, Evie wrote a fresh letter to her brother.

Dear Albert,

Please tell me you're coming home. That you're still alive, somewhere. Maybe you think right now that it would be better that you weren't, like Corporal Higa says, but he also says it gets better, and I have to believe it does, too. Come home to us.

Love,
Evie

Evie didn't bother putting the letter in an envelope. She set it aside on her table and stumbled to her bed to drift into an uneasy sleep.

Chapter Eight

THE NEXT MORNING, Evie found her desk just as she left it. She finished typing up a few reports before making the rounds with Lieutenant Mead. Glenn was away from the ward. She told herself it didn't matter, but she kept glancing toward the door, wondering when the men would come back from their therapy sessions.

After lunch, Major Rosenbach had her take another stack of reports to the lab. Evie eagerly accepted the assignment. She delivered the reports to an unfamiliar nurse.

The girl looked through them and shook her head. "These doctors use penicillin like we're never going to run out."

"*Are* we going to run out?" Evie asked.

"Not as long as we're careful about who gets it. But lately we've been coming up short for some reason, and they can barely make enough to keep up with the demand as it is."

The nurse gave her a nod and strode away. Evie stood very still, watching the quiet bustle of the lab. The work that these men and women did, peering into microscopes and studying blood smears on glass plates—none of it was secret. Everyone knew now that penicillin was the wonder drug. But not everyone *had* penicillin. The US barely had enough of it for their troops and the occasional civilian case. Britain had some, but Germany had only the tiny amount it could steal from captured Allied doctors or soldiers, and Japan had none. It was the US that led the way in making the wonder drug, but it was still rationed here, along with fuel and chocolate and stockings. A precious commodity. Precious enough to steal.

Evie backed into the hallway, her mind too full to process everything at once. The doctors had used penicillin on Corporal Higa and on Private Smith—and Smith's surgery had been delayed because they were short of the wonder drug. What if it wasn't the information in the files that someone was after? What if a spy was trying to steal some of the actual drug? The hospital kept the penicillin locked up until it was time to use it. The thief would need to know when and where it was going to be used next, which they could learn from patient files. But someone would have to look an ill or wounded man in the eyes—one who had sacrificed his all for his country—and be willing to take away the thing that would make him better. Would anyone do that?

Maybe.

Maybe if they were more loyal to another country, or to someone who would pay well enough for the drug.

Evie walked back to her desk at a fast clip. She had to find out who could steal the penicillin and when they might strike again.

She hurried back to her ward and took up her station at her typewriter. She stared at the blank sheet of paper and the shorthand notes waiting for her, then glanced into Major Rosenbach's office. She should tell him, but he was so distracted, and he never took her seriously. She would have to prove penicillin was going missing or that someone was going to take it before she took it to Major Rosenbach.

Or what if his recent distraction was because *he* was the one taking it? How could she know?

"Miss Lewis! Come play ping pong with us!" Glenn and two other patients beckoned to her from outside her office.

"Maybe later."

Glenn glanced at his watch. "Okay, it's later now."

She hesitated, but here was her chance to find out more. Lieutenant Mead encouraged her to talk to the boys. And Glenn's eyes laughed at her.

"I hate to show you all up," she said, "but if you insist."

The three young men laughed and escorted her down the ward to the covered porch with the ping pong table. Corporal Higa sat up in bed, playing a Hawaiian tune on his guitar. He paused as they walked by.

"Hey, don't keep Miss Lewis all to yourself!"

"You know what they say about early birds," Glenn shot back with a grin.

"Miss Lewis, if he's calling you a worm, I can promise you I'm more of a gentleman. How about a game of checkers later?"

"Sure thing," she said.

On the screened porch, they picked up the ping pong paddles and paired off. Evie was a little disappointed to find herself facing off against Glenn, but then his challenging smile stirred her competitive edge.

"Don't expect me to take it easy on you fellows," she said.

"Of course not," Glenn said. "I'm only missing one hand, and Terry here is great with his hooks."

Terry grinned and tossed the ping pong paddle from one hooked prosthesis to the other. Evie raised an eyebrow in appreciation.

"You and Ray have all your hands intact," Terry said. "That gives you a disadvantage, but we'll try not to stomp you too hard."

Ray, one of the few black patients in the ward, laughed and shifted his weight on his artificial leg. "Oh, we'll see about that, won't we Miss Lewis?"

"Yes, no quarter given."

"And none asked for," Glenn said, serving the ball.

The game continued at a fast clip. Evie hardly had to do anything but hit the ball when it bounced right at her. Ray's false leg didn't slow him down at all, and Terry and Glenn almost never missed a shot. Finally, though, Ray hit a decisive shot, and Glenn missed the return, putting Ray and Evie as the winners.

Ray shook Evie's hand enthusiastically, then he looked slightly horrified at his familiarity.

She smiled reassuringly. "Good game, sir!"

Ray relaxed and turned back to Glenn and Terry. "Now, you boys have to pay up."

"Pay up?" Evie asked.

"Losers have to buy the winners milkshakes at the PX."

"No time like the present," Glenn said.

Evie glanced at her watch, but she wasn't pressed for time. She shrugged. "If you insist."

They walked back through the ward, the boys surrounding her. She felt an odd mix of protectiveness toward them and reassurance at their presence.

"That was some game, Miss Lewis," Terry said. "Your fellow's one lucky guy."

Glenn, to Evie's left, tensed a little.

"My fellow?" Evie asked.

"Glenn said you've got a fellow in the fight."

"Oh! You must mean my brother, Albert," she said quietly.

"Your-your brother?" Glenn asked, and Terry elbowed him with a grin.

Evie gave him a curious look. "Yes. But I hope he *is* lucky. I hope the Japanese haven't taken him."

They walked a short distance in sympathetic silence. She could feel it—the understanding that these young men had for her worries—and it wrapped around the aching part of her and seemed to whisper that her deep and vulnerable wound was safe with them. A faint tingle rolled down the back of her scalp, and a tension she hadn't even been aware of loosened enough for her to take a deeper breath. How long had it been since she'd felt safe or supported? Maybe only with Robbie. She squeezed her eyes shut for a moment to stop any tears from coming and opened them to find Glenn watching her with sympathy.

"We'll all pray for him," Ray said with conviction.

Evie smiled at the thought of prayers from different voices and different faiths going up in Albert's behalf. It might or might not bring him home, but it was all they could do from where they were.

"Thank you," Evie said quietly.

Their mood lightened somewhat when they reached the PX. Evie did a quick scan of the candy bars. Plenty of Forever Yours but no Milky Ways. Was it a sign? No, she couldn't afford to think that way. Glenn and Terry ordered their milkshakes and looked to Evie.

"I'll have chocolate," she said.

"Excellent choice," Glenn said.

They sat and talked about their ward's chances of winning the Christmas decoration contest and Helen Keller's upcoming visit as they sipped their milkshakes. Evie glanced around at their faces. There was something old in their eyes at times, but at the moment they were just young men enjoying a treat. Even Terry, with two hook hands, had no trouble chugging his straw up and down to break up the ice cream and sipping down the shake. And Ray sat next to her—something that would be impossible in most restaurants in Utah or the rest of the country, where Ray would not be welcome. Nor would Corporal Higa. What a strange and wonderful world Bushnell was.

"Good milkshake?" Glenn asked. "You've got such a dreamy smile, I'd swear you do have a fellow out there somewhere."

"I was just thinking what a swell place this hospital is."

"I'll drink to that!" Terry raised his glass in a toast, and the others joined him.

They returned to their shakes, and Evie's thoughts continued to wander.

"It's like watching a stormy afternoon," Glenn said.

"What?"

"Now you're frowning like you're facing down all the world's problems."

"Maybe you should pay more attention to your milkshake."

"But your mouth is much more interesting," Glenn said.

Evie raised an eyebrow, expecting him to back down, but he just returned her daring gaze.

Ray whistled. "Cool it down, you two."

Glenn laughed. "I have to practice my flirting. The way I'm coming with my prostheses, I'll be out of here not long after Terry."

"Are you leaving soon?" Evie asked Terry.

"I already got to go home on a visit. Everything went well, so I'm hoping they let me out in time for Christmas."

"That's wonderful," Evie said.

She hoped wherever Albert was that he would get to celebrate Christmas too.

"There, now you're frowning again," Glenn said quietly while Ray and Terry talked about their homes in California.

"Christmas is hard."

Glenn nodded. "It can be. But it's about hope."

"For something in the future." Evie punched her straw into the milkshake. "Something we might not ever reach."

"Sometimes hope can be its own thing. Right now, in the present."

"The present! The present has its own problems."

"Do you want to talk about them?" Glenn asked quietly.

Evie started to shake her head then met his eyes. He saw a lot of what was going on in the ward. He and the other soldiers had a vested interest in making sure no spies were lurking about. But Major Rosenbach hadn't believed her.

"You'll probably laugh at me."

"It's possible, but why not give me a shot?" He touched her hand, sending a thrill over her skin, then quickly pulled away.

Evie sighed. "Do you remember the day we met?"

"How could I forget? I still have bruises. No, don't look like that. I'm joking. What about it?"

"Remember how I asked you about the missing file?"

"Yeah."

"I think someone took it. And then I think they took other files."

"Did you tell the doctor?"

"Major Rosenbach is unconcerned. But he's seemed distracted lately."

"Hmm." Glenn glanced at Terry and Ray, who were still distracted by their own conversation. "We've noticed that too. He hasn't smiled in ages."

"I can't prove it, but I think someone's trying to find out about penicillin so they can steal it. The nurse in the lab said they've been coming up short."

She studied Glenn's face for even a twitch of amusement, but he watched her with serious concern.

"You believe me?" she asked.

"I believe it's possible. I've seen what the wonder drug can do, and it's in short supply out there."

Evie leaned forward. "Will you help me find out?"

"Find out what?" Terry asked.

"Miss Lewis thinks someone's trying to take some of the penicillin."

"That's awful!" Ray said. "Who?"

"That's what we need to find out." Glenn turned back to Evie. "Do you have any ideas?"

The men watched her expectantly. "There are a few people who have been acting strangely. Major Rosenbach for one, but I can hardly imagine—"

"Right now, we're just talking about ideas," Glenn said. "You're not accusing anyone, so you don't need to defend them either."

Evie nodded. "Lieutenant Mead disappears at odd times. Then there's that POW that cleans the ward."

"Not Paolo!" Terry said. "He's a hoot."

Evie glared. "I'm not accusing anyone, just throwing out ideas. He has access to the ward, and... I know it sounds strange, but I thought I saw him at the dance the other night."

The men exchanged a guilty look.

"What?" Evie asked.

"It's possible you did see him at the dance," Terry said.

"What!" Evie scooted back. Were these men all conspiring together?

Terry sighed. "Paolo's our buddy. He missed... well, he missed talking to girls and drinking sodas and having fun. It's not actually so hard for those POWs to sneak out of their barracks if they have anywhere to go."

"But their clothes..." The PW painted on their shirts and pants made them stand out.

"I had an extra uniform," Ray admitted. "Paolo's about the same size as me."

Evie leaned back and glared at all of them. "You may have been helping an enemy spy! What were you thinking?"

"Ah, Miss Lewis, think about it," Glenn said. "The Italians are out of the war now. Paolo and the others are waiting for the fighting to end so they can go home. He's just a guy like us."

"I'm surprised you can say that," Evie said. "Wasn't it the Italians who—" she gestured at his missing arm.

Glenn glanced down at his prosthetic hook and shrugged. "Yeah, I suppose it was. I'm pretty sure it wasn't Paolo who threw the grenade, though."

Terry chuckled, and Glenn went on.

"Even if it was, he was just doing what he was commanded to do like the rest of us. There are some maniacs over there in Germany, running the show. Probably some petty tyrants in the ranks too. But a lot of those fellows don't want to be fighting. They're just trying to survive and see their families again like the rest of us."

Terry and Ray nodded. Evie studied all of them.

"Well, Paolo doesn't have access after-hours anyway, unless you guys are sneaking him into the ward after we leave."

"Nah, we've never done that," Terry said. "It was just that one dance."

"He even gave the uniform back," Ray said.

"I still think there's something suspicious about him," Evie said.

"Anyone else?" Glenn asked.

Evie thought about it. "Not really. Well, when I told the tech sergeant down in the labs about the missing folder, he seemed almost too unconcerned about it.

"And there are always nurses wandering around," Ray added. "And mechanics and folks like that when something breaks."

"True, but let's start with what we have," Glenn said. "Would any of these people have a reason to steal medicine? A connection to anyone overseas, maybe?"

They all looked at each other. Terry flicked his cigarette and shrugged.

"We need to find out more," Evie said. "It might look suspicious if we start questioning people."

"Not if we spread it out," Glenn said. "One of us asks a question here, another asks one there."

"Let's decide what we're going to ask, then," Evie said, and they huddled down into a whispered conference around their milkshakes.

Chapter Nine

EVIE'S FIRST ASSIGNMENT was to find out more about Lieutenant Mead as she took notes for him the next day. Glenn and the others filed out for their morning therapy sessions, and Glenn made eye contact with her and gave her a slow wink. She rolled her eyes. As if this was just a game to him. But he took her seriously enough to try to find out if there were any rumors about missing penicillin in the other wards.

Evie accompanied Lieutenant Mead as he visited Private Smith. While the therapist went over his notes, Evie sat by the silent patient and chatted. She studied the young man's face. He didn't look at her, but his jaw was clenched, and his eyes were wide. Evie remembered what Corporal Higa had said about needing assurance regarding the present. But what could she say about it? Even if the future was hazy, it seemed so full of potential promises, a mirage that she was always trying to catch up with.

"Do you think our ward will win the decorating contest?" she asked Private Smith. "I like how the boys have done it up."

He actually looked at her this time, his eyes questioning.

"The lights are my favorite part," Evie said. "This time of year gets so dark and grey sometimes, but I love the bright reds and greens. It almost seems like a reason for the sun to go down earlier, so we can see all these other colors."

Private Smith still didn't answer her, but his eyes traced the strings of lights hanging by the doorway, and his face relaxed a little.

Lieutenant Mead examined Smith's healing sutures and shook his head. "I think we may need to take more of the stump off before we can fit you with a prosthetic. Miss Lewis, please visit with the patient for a few minutes while I check on something."

He stood very still for a moment then paced out of the room. Evie watched him go. Another surgery meant the chance at another dose of penicillin. She rose to follow him, but Private Smith grabbed her hand.

Lieutenant Mead's white coat disappeared out the front door. Evie pulled to follow him but looked back at Smith's anxious face, the silent appeal in his eyes. Slowly, she took her seat again.

"Do I have to?" Private Smith asked.

"Have to?" Evie repeated.

"Have another surgery?" His eyes were large, and Evie wondered how old he was. He should have been at least eighteen, but some boys lied about their age to join up. "These doctors are going to keep chopping me up a little bit at a time."

"I suppose you don't have to agree if you don't want a prosthetic leg."

He stared straight ahead. "I doubt I'll be able to do what those other guys do anyway."

"Why do you think that?"

"They're running around playing basketball and ping pong and going swimming and dancing, and I can barely sit up."

"But you *can* sit up, and you're getting stronger. Even I can see that."

"Really?"

"Well, sure. You move yourself better than you did before, and there's a healthier look to your face."

"Yeah?"

"Yeah. More color, and it's more filled out."

"Well, I eat better here than in New Guinea!" His face fell. "But I'm never going to catch up with those other guys."

"You don't have to. Not yet. You just have to be a little stronger than you were the day before. It's like, if you were trying to hike those mountains out there," she gestured out the window, "and you just looked at the tops, it might seem too far, but if you just look at the next stopping point or switchback in the trail, you can take it one stage at a time."

Private Smith stared out the window for a quiet moment.

"It was like that in battle," he whispered. "I couldn't really see where we were headed or what we were trying to do, but little by little we took back the islands."

Evie held her breath, hoping the thoughts of war didn't press him back into to silence. He stared out the window for some time, then looked at Evie, his eyes serious. "I made it through that one day at a time. I guess I can do this too."

"Of course, you can!" Evie squeezed his hand, and he grinned at her, looking very much like a boy again.

They chatted about his home and parents until Lieutenant Mead came back. He looked surprised at the change in Private Smith and gave Evie a nod of appreciation.

Later, Corporal Higa motioned her aside.

"You did a good thing for Private Smith."

Evie shrugged. "I just talked to him."

"You treated him like a person. Every guy in here, no matter how tough or happy-go-lucky he acts, is terrified of how he's going to be treated when he leaves here. You're kind of a bridge between them and that world out there that scares them."

"Is the world going to be kind to them, do you think? It's different here in Brigham City, where people are used to it, but out there..."

"People can be cruel when someone is different, but I think this war has opened people's eyes to things beyond what they're used to seeing."

"What are you going to do?" Evie asked.

Higa smiled. "I'm just taking life one day at a time. They're having meatloaf for dinner tonight. I like meatloaf."

Evie laughed.

"Hey, did you hear about the Bushnell baby?"

"No," Evie said. "Did Jeannie have her baby?"

"I don't know the mother's name, but I heard we have a new arrival."

"I'll have to go check on her tonight."

Chapter Ten

EVIE TRIED TO follow Lieutenant Mead after work, but he slipped away too quickly. Instead, she made the trip through the long hallways to the sectioned off ward that served as a maternity area. Evie thought there would only be one baby, but she could hear several cries echoing off the walls. Nurses hurried about with food trays and blankets, and Evie practically had to waylay one of them to get directions. She gave a start when she recognized the Japanese nurse from the bus.

"I'm here to see Jeannie Harding," Evie said, regaining her composure. "She just had her baby. I'm a friend."

"Thank goodness!" The nurse brushed back a loose strand of black hair. "They ordered her husband back to his ward to rest, so she needs a friend right now. Right over there."

Evie tiptoed to the curtained-off area the nurse indicated. There was no way to knock, so she softly called, "Jeannie?"

"Yes?" called a strained voice.

Evie stuck her head in. Jeannie cradled a crying infant, her hair tangled and her eyes rimmed with red.

"Oh, Miss Lewis, how kind of you to come." Jeannie wiped her eyes with the back of her free hand and tried on a watery smile.

"What's wrong, dear?" Evie's worst fears were relieved by the movements of the baby.

"Our baby," Jeannie said quietly. "She has a hernia. Her intestine... she needs surgery."

"Oh, I'm so sorry." Evie sat in a wooden chair next to Jeannie's bed. "Bushnell has some of the best surgeons in the country. Are they going to do the surgery here?"

"They want to, but they need m-more medicine."

"Medicine?" Evie asked, a chill prickling down her spine.

"That new wonder drug. They had permission to use it for my baby, but now they've come up short. Without it, there's a risk of infection. But if she doesn't have the surgery, she can't digest her food."

"Oh, honey." Evie wrapped an arm around Jeannie's shoulder. Her stomach churned, and she swallowed down her nausea. Was she too late already? "Are they sending for more penicillin?"

"Yes, but they said it takes time." Jeannie gently stroked her baby's cheek.

Evie nodded. They'd gotten faster, but growing the penicillin mold was still a painfully slow process when so many lives depended on it.

"I'll do what I can," Evie said.

Jeannie gave her a confused look. "What can you do?"

Evie repressed a groan. She shouldn't tell Jeannie that someone might be taking the penicillin. The new mother already had enough worries. "I know some of the doctors and technicians here. I'll talk to them."

Jeannie nodded, but her eyes were dull.

"You should get some rest," Evie said.

Jeannie shook her head. "I want every minute with her. Just in case." New tears welled in her eyes.

Evie offered Jeannie hollow comforts before saying her farewells and marching out. She scanned the room for the nurses, but they seemed to be busy elsewhere. She thought about the Japanese nurse. Could the woman be a spy, stealing medicine for the Japanese? Even if not, she might know something about the missing medicine.

Evie checked in the ward offices but didn't see her. Then she looked out in the hall.

The Japanese nurse sat on a bench with her knees pulled up and her head down. Evie wondered for a moment if the nurse had fallen asleep, but then the woman's shoulders trembled silently.

"Miss?" Evie asked.

The nurse jumped and looked up at Evie, dabbing her eyes with a handkerchief. "Sorry, I didn't hear you there. I mean—"

"Are you okay?" Evie asked. Spy or no spy, her heart went out to the woman trying to wipe away her tears.

"I'm just...I didn't get dinner, and now I don't have time to go down to the PX."

Evie felt a twinge of empathy. How often had she worked too long and missed dinner? She felt in her handbag and pulled out Glenn's Forever Yours bar.

"Would this help?"

The nurse nodded, but her face remained bleak, cast into an unhealthy color by the flickering light overhead.

"Can I share it with you?" Evie asked on an impulse. The dim corridor seemed lonely—too lonely for anyone to eat alone. "I didn't get anything for dinner either."

The nurse brightened up a little and nodded.

"I'm Mary," the nurse said.

"Evie."

She sat next to Mary on the polished wood bench and split the candy bar, giving Mary the bigger half. They ate in silence, letting the dark chocolate melt on their tongues while *Joy to the World* played on a radio in the background.

"This is so good," Mary said.

Evie nodded. Why had she been waiting so long to enjoy it?

"I don't usually miss dinner." Mary discreetly licked some chocolate off the end of her finger. "I went into town with some of the other nurses, but..." She sighed and stared out the window at the darkening sky.

"What happened?" Evie asked.

"The restaurant wouldn't let me in. They said, 'No dogs or Japs.'"

Evie gritted her teeth. "That's terrible!"

"I'm from here in Box Elder County, you know," Mary said as if she couldn't hear Evie. She was just speaking to exorcise her ghosts. "I was born maybe ten miles south of here. I've eaten in *that* restaurant before. But even with my nurse's uniform, they turned me away."

"That shouldn't happen!" Evie said. But hadn't she just wondered if the young woman might be a spy, just because she looked Japanese? And on the bus, Evie hadn't spoken in her defense. No one had been brave enough to, except the driver.

"Everything was better before Pearl Harbor," Mary whispered. "I don't know if it will ever be right again."

Evie opened her mouth but had no words for Mary's experience. What would Corporal Higa say? Something about liking meatloaf, no doubt.

Evie put her hand on Mary's. "Thank you for helping Jeannie."

Mary smiled a little and nodded. "I love working with the mothers and babies. I think I have the best job at Bushnell. Some of the soldiers would...would get almost hysterical if I tried to help them." She swallowed hard. "I guess I can understand. But babies don't care."

They chatted until Mary's break was over. Evie watched her go back into the ward then leaned her head against the wall and watched the dark blue sky outside the window fade to black. How was anyone supposed to find their way when they were just stumbling in the dark?

The hospital was quieter at night, with a smaller staff on duty. But if someone was stealing from the hospital, wouldn't this be the time to do it? Evie stood. The hospital was just so *big*—a small city in itself. She needed help. She hurried back to her ward. At least Glenn and the other men would still be there.

On her way into the ward, she nearly slammed into Major Rosenbach.

"Major! I'm sorry."

His monumental eyebrows rose even higher. "Miss Lewis. Why are you back?"

"I forgot...my key."

"Should I help you look?" He turned back half-heartedly.

"No, go ahead. I think I know where I left it."

"Just as well. I need to go home and light another candle on the menorah with my wife."

"Oh, yes! Happy Hanukkah."

He shook his head. "It's usually a happy time. But this year... I can't seem to enjoy it."

Evie had been looking past him, trying to spot Glenn, Terry, or Ray. His tone made her turn more fully to him.

"I'm sorry to hear that." She let a question hang in her voice.

"We're hearing reports of what's happening in Germany." He looked to the east, dark circles hanging under his eyes. "I have cousins who live there still. I don't know what's happened to them, but if the rumors are to be believed..." He gave her a sad half-smile. "It is not a Happy Hanukkah for the Jews in Germany."

"No, it wouldn't be."

"I'm afraid I haven't been a good boss lately. This is the Festival of Lights, but the news each day is so grey, it's a burden just getting out of bed. I know these boys fought hard and deserve my best, but I don't have it to give."

"You're human too," Evie said. "You're doing the best you can. We all are."

"Thank you, dear. Good night." He patted her shoulder and put on his brown felt fedora before walking heavily down the corridor.

Evie hurried past the night guard, who was reading the *Saturday Evening Post*, and found Glenn, Terry, and Ray playing poker with Corporal Higa.

"Miss Lewis." Glenn rose to his feet.

Evie pulled a chair over and sat next to Glenn. "Did any of you find anything useful today?"

He shook his head.

"You heard about the baby born here?" Evie asked. "Well, she needs a surgery, but they said they've come up short on their penicillin supply."

"You think it's been stolen?" Glenn asked.

Evie nodded.

Glenn muttered a curse under his breath. "Sorry for the language, Miss Lewis."

She waved away his apology. "What are we going to do? We need to stop this before someone dies."

"Who's going to die?" Corporal Higa asked, pushing his wheelchair closer.

Evie glanced around the room. There could be a spy at Bushnell, but she trusted these men. They were part of the Bushnell family. "I think someone's been stealing penicillin. The... the Bushnell Baby needs it, or she may die. And the soldiers here need it as well."

A few other men gathered around. Private Smith forced himself to a sitting position in his bed and leaned forward. Evie quickly outlined what she knew.

"I don't think Major Rosenbach is a likely suspect anymore. He's mourning his family in Germany and has no reason to help

Hitler. But we have to be careful who knows about this. We don't want the thief to know we're watching for him."

"So, we're doing counter-espionage?" Corporal Higa asked. "Spying to catch the spy?"

"Exactly! Anything that seems strange we report to each other."

The men broke into smaller groups, comparing notes on various doctors, therapists, and nurses. Glenn watched them with a serious expression.

"What are you thinking?" Evie asked.

"It's Friday. A lot of the staff won't be around until Monday, and if your friend's baby needs that medicine now..."

"We'll find it. We have to."

Glenn shook his head. "Some things are out of your hands, you know."

Evie stood. "Aren't you the one who's always talking about hope?"

"Sure, it's good to keep up hope, but hope can hurt sometimes, like when you're hoping for someone to live, and it's already... Well, sometimes you just have to trust God and let things go."

"I'm not going to give up."

"But you can't take on everything yourself."

"At least I take it seriously!" Evie glared at him. "Though that's not something I would expect you to understand."

Glenn's eyes narrowed, and he turned his back on her. Evie stormed out of the ward. Glenn was wrong. Wrong, wrong, wrong. She would help Jeannie and her baby. She would help Albert. Everything was going to be okay. Just a little longer and all of this would be sorted out.

The lab technicians often worked late. There was at least one suspect she could investigate now. She made her way down the stark, white hallways to the lab. Most of the lights in the room were off, but one bulb shone a jaundiced yellow into the hall.

She peeked in. Sergeant Meyers was alone, but he glanced nervously over his shoulder from time to time, the light glinting off his glasses. He rubbed a polishing cloth over one of the microscopes. It might have been his normal Friday evening routine, but his shoulders were hunched like he was afraid of being noticed.

Evie backed into the shadows to watch him. He soon had the last microscope put in place, and with a hasty glance at his wristwatch, he turned out the light and swept right past her hiding place in the shadows and down the hall.

Those cursed long halls. Other than the doorways, they gave few places to hide. Luckily, the tech sergeant seemed intent on hurrying somewhere.

Evie took off her boots and stole quietly down the dim, silent hallways. The floor was icy cold against her bare feet and she wished for her forbidden stockings. Once the tech sergeant paused to listen, and she pressed against a doorway and prayed that she looked like part of the shadows. He turned a corner—the same one where she had crashed into Glenn. They had installed a mirror there so she could see around the corner.

The tech sergeant headed for a doorway and out into the moonless night. Evie snuck after him, the chill outside sending goose bumps over her skin, and her breath clouding the air until she hid it behind her hand.

She lost the tech sergeant in the rows of identical tan brick buildings. Noise and lights poured from the windows in the wards, but he was nowhere to be seen. Evie slunk forward, staying in the shadows.

A hand grabbed her and covered her mouth. She tried to scream, but the grip tightened. She bit into the palm and kicked back. A male voice oomphed in the darkness, and she scrambled forward, but someone tripped up her feet. She went sprawling, tumbling down a low incline of frost-covered brown grass. Before she could get up, a sharp knee pinned her face-down.

"Why are you following me?" Sergeant Meyers asked. "Are you a spy?"

She shook her head against the pressure of his hand forcing her lips against her teeth.

"Don't try to lie to me. I know you followed me out of the building, and carrying your shoes so you could sneak. Who do you work for?"

Evie could try to scream. There were guards around. But he was covering her nose too, and she was starting to feel light-headed.

She spoke into his hand, trying to get him to move it.

"What?" He lifted his fingers slightly.

She sucked in a long, icy breath. "I'm not a spy. I'm trying to figure out who's stealing the penicillin."

Sergeant Meyers leaned back, though he kept Evie pinned down. "This is about the penicillin? We have been coming up short."

"Someone stole it," Evie said.

"Are you sure?"

Evie nodded. "It wasn't you?"

"No! Of course not. I thought *you* were up to something." He released the pressure on her. She pulled her legs under her and wiggled away from him, but he didn't seem to notice. His face pinched in perplexed thought. "That would explain why we keep coming up short. We thought someone had just been careless."

"Who could have taken it?" Evie asked. "We need to stop them."

"I-I don't know," Sergeant Meyers shook his head.

"Then why have you been sneaking around?"

He looked over his shoulder.

Evie backed further away and got into a sprinter's pose. "If I scream for a guard—"

"Okay, wait!" He sank back into the grass. "I'm dating someone. I was on my way to meet her tonight."

"Why is that a problem?"

"I'm a sergeant. She's a nurse—a second lieutenant."

Evie remembered the platinum blonde from the movies. "Nurses can't date non-commissioned officers."

He nodded miserably. "I don't want her to get in trouble. I just want this war to be over so we can be together."

Evie watched his face. He could be lying. A very good actor. But she doubted it. That left Lieutenant Mead. Or someone else she hadn't even identified yet.

"You'd best go see her, then," Evie said.

"Thank you."

Sergeant Meyers pushed his glasses up and hurried off into the darkness. Evie shivered as the damp cold of the grass seeped through her skirt. She wrapped her arms around her knees and lowered her head. Who was she trying to fool? Maybe Glenn was right, and she was in over her head.

She fumbled for her boots and shoved them on her numbed feet then wandered back toward the women's housing. The stars glittered in the cold above, aloof and uncaring. Whatever answers they had, they weren't sharing.

She got back to the room she shared with Fran, surprised to find the lights still on.

"You didn't have to wait up for me," she said as she hung up her coat.

Then she saw the look of fear in Fran's eyes. Her friend held up the yellow envelope of a telegram with Evie's name on it.

Chapter Eleven

EVIE BACKED AWAY from the bold words *Western Union*. The lines to the hospital telephone exchange were always busy, and she had no phone of her own, so a telegram was the surest way for her family to get a message to her if they needed to tell her something important. Something dreadful.

"I can't. Oh, Fran. I can't open it."

"It could be good news."

Evie squeezed her eyes closed. As long as she stood there, shutting out the light of the room, with the telegram sealed, whatever news it contained didn't have to be true. She could stay busy and keep shoving her fears off for another time.

But her parents or Robbie would eventually get through to the telephone exchange or even come to see her about the news, whatever it was. The truth was a crushing avalanche too large and fast for her to hide from.

"Open it for me, please." Evie forced herself to watch as Fran tore the envelope and pulled out the paper. Her friend read it twice, then looked up, her eyes wide.

"Well?" The word rasped from Evie's throat.

"It's from your parents," Fran whispered. "The army found Albert's plane."

Evie sat heavily. "His plane."

A POW, then? It was terrible, but it might mean there was still hope.

"Parts of it. The wreckage. In the mountains. And the body of at least one of the crew members. They're still working on identifying...everything."

"Oh."

Evie just stared. Fran might have called her name, but it was fuzzy, like she was underwater. Drowning. None of it was real. Albert was fine. He was coming home soon. His plane wasn't in pieces scattered across a mountain range in China or India.

Fran guided her to bed. Evie curled up, still fully dressed, clutching her blanket to her chest. Fran softly turned out the light, and the mattress across the room creaked lightly as Fran went to bed.

Evie stared into the darkness. A night without stars. Blackness without any sign of light. Slowly, the tears welled and dripped onto her pillow, soaking the cotton against her cheek. She still made no sound and watched the darkness as it passed, turning away only when light began to creep across the window.

There was no reason to get up the next morning. It was Saturday. Evie wasn't hungry. There was nothing she could do that mattered.

Fran brought her back a pastry from breakfast, or perhaps lunch, but Evie couldn't manage to eat it. She dozed a little and woke feeling sticky and stiff.

"Into the bath with you," Fran said.

"Why?"

Fran settled on the bed next to her and stroked her hair back. "You have every right to hurt, sweetie, but you have to take care of yourself too. Your brother would want you to."

Evie winced but forced herself to sit up. "Okay."

"I'd like you to come with me tonight too."

"What's tonight?"

"Helen Keller."

Evie groaned. "I don't think I can stand all the crowds and another celebrity trying to cheer everyone up. Not tonight."

"This isn't just another celebrity. This is Helen Keller. I've always admired her. You're not going to get many chances in your life to hear from someone like that."

"I'll think about it."

Evie stumbled into the bathroom and twisted the tub's brass handle. Hot water poured down, filling the room with steam. She slipped off her dirty blouse and skirt and stepped into the bath. The warmth cradled her. She thought of Jeannie's baby. She thought of Albert, crashing alone on some snow-covered mountain top. Had he suffered, or had it been quick? Had he been cold? Evie curled around herself and prayed. *Please, God, don't let Albert have died in the cold.*

And then the tears came, hot, shaking her whole body. She kept the water running, letting it pour over her legs and drain out, and she sobbed and sobbed until she was empty inside. She ducked her face under the faucet, and the water felt colder than her tears. Her eyes stung from crying, but she cleaned her face.

She would find out more about what happened to Albert. There might not be hope, but there was still a chance to understand. She stood and dried off, feeling like a mortician preparing a corpse for a viewing—everything bleak and lifeless.

But she slipped on a fresh gray blouse and black skirt and went through the motions of brushing her hair out and tying a scarf over it. She could go to see Helen Keller for Fran. Her mind was so distant and lost, it didn't matter much where her body was.

They filed into the Red Cross auditorium with hundreds of soldiers, all in uniform. Some walked, but many came on crutches or in wheelchairs. Evie glanced around for Glenn, then remembered that he probably didn't want to talk to her, and she wasn't sure she wanted to talk to him either.

She and Fran found seats on the outside edge of the group. A man walked onto the stage and spoke about Helen Keller: the fever that took her sight and hearing at a young age, and how a persistent teacher and friend pulled her from her dark and silent world. She eventually learned to communicate and went on to get her education and become an activist for those with disabilities.

The crowd hushed as Helen Keller walked out with her assistant and addressed the crowd. Evie leaned forward. Helen Keller's voice was a little unsteady, even with the microphone, but her assistant clarified her message of hope and happiness. Evie flinched from it, but the words chased her into the gloomy corners of her misery.

Miss Keller knew the darkness and promised there was beauty even in its black stillness. She didn't shy away from talking of suffering in a room full of people who knew what that meant. She challenged them to find the joy and triumph in overcoming obstacles, to look past momentary failures to the happiness of tomorrow, but also to find the wonder in where they were right at that moment.

The words jolted Evie. How much of her life had she spent waiting for tomorrow to be better? After Christmas, after Albert came home, after the war was over. She'd been so busy looking forward to later that she hadn't taken a moment to enjoy what was right in front of her. She sank down in misery under the weight of realizing how much happiness and wonder she must have let slip by unnoticed, never to be reclaimed.

But Miss Keller's reassurances wrapped around Evie and pulled her up, reminding her she could start again, right that moment. When Miss Keller said that the things we love are never lost, tears spilled down Evie's cheeks. Not hot and harrowing, but warm, soft. Albert would never be gone from her. She had to keep going for him, too, because his journey would continue with her and the work that she did.

Miss Keller invited a pretty young girl to come up and play the piano so she could sing along. Evie craned to see. How could someone who couldn't see or hear sing along with a piano?

Miss Keller put her hand on the piano and motioned for the girl to begin playing. She did, the folksy notes of "Home of the Range" echoing through the silent hall.

And Helen Keller sang. It was perhaps not the most musically perfect rendition performed in that hall, but tears once again prickled Evie's eyes as the blind and deaf woman, guided only by the vibrations from the piano, sang the well-known song.

When she was done, the hall broke into applause. Miss Keller smiled. Evie wondered if she could feel the vibration of the clapping, the gratitude and admiration of the men and women listening to her, the echoes of the hope she had instilled in them.

A young man in a wheelchair nearby whispered to his companion, "I feel like all of my troubles are nothing now."

Evie nodded to herself. Her troubles were still there, but they did not seem insurmountable. She would make Albert proud. She would find the person who was stealing the penicillin and risking the lives of the patients at Bushnell.

Chapter Twelve

IT HAD TO be Lieutenant Mead. The whole walk over to work on Monday, Evie buzzed with conviction. Today, she would work with Mead, and when he scurried out for one of his secret meetings, she would catch him. She tore through her typing in record time and was ready when Lieutenant Mead came for her.

"We have a new patient today," he said. "Just came in on the train this weekend."

Evie nodded and followed him, carrying her notebook and pencil. The young man had a bandage over part of his face, and he was missing most of his arm, but he smiled back when Evie gave him an encouraging grin.

Lieutenant Mead made some brief remarks about the condition of the young man's stump, then slipped away toward the hall while Evie wrote down her notes. She quietly excused herself and snuck out after him.

Lieutenant Mead was hunched over a wastebasket in the hallway, heaving his breakfast into the receptacle. Evie gasped a little, and he looked up, his expression pale and chagrinned.

"It's shameful, I know," he said.

"Lieutenant?"

"I can't handle it. The raw flesh, the talk of blood and death. I'm a physical therapist. I'm trained to help people learn to walk again, not to look at maggoty—"

He threw up again. Evie knelt next to him on the cold tile, uncertain how to help.

He groaned. "I wanted to do my part. They needed therapists. But I'm a joke."

"No, you're not," Evie said, handing him a handkerchief that she would definitely not want back. "You're helping those young men in there. None of us knew what we were getting involved in when we started working here, but think of all the soldiers able to get around now because of you."

He smiled weakly. "Thank you. I, uh, hope you won't let this get around."

Evie smiled back. "Our little secret."

But if he was running outside to empty his stomach, he probably wasn't having secret meeting with a spy at the same time. All of her suspects were looking less likely. Despair threatened to swallow her, but she forced herself to pull away from it. Someone was taking the penicillin. She would find out who.

"More bad day, mister doctor?" Paolo asked, taking the waste bin.

Lieutenant Mead nodded miserably, apparently no longer concerned about the rule of not talking to the POWs. Paolo helped the lieutenant back to his feet. The Italian looked at Evie, all trace of joking gone from his face.

"You do your desk safe?"

"Pardon?" Evie glanced at Lieutenant Mead, but he didn't seem interested in stopping the forbidden conversation.

"The reasonment I try to say you. Your desk not safe."

"My desk. My papers! Have you seen someone going through them?"

Paolo nodded. "Sì!"

"Who?"

"Hmm. Lady. Is nurse."

"A nurse! What did she look like?"

"Has white hairs."

"She's old?"

"No, no, no. Yellow hairs. Like you. Whiter."

"Oh, blonde! Very light blonde?"

Paolo nodded. A prickle ran down Evie's spine. Very light blonde, like Sergeant Meyers' nurse. But there were plenty of blondes at Bushnell.

"Anything else?"

He shrugged and smiled sheepishly. "Pretty. She no marry me neither."

"I'm sure you'll find your girl someday. But will you tell me if you see the nurse again?"

"Sì!"

Evie filled Lieutenant Mead and Major Rosenbach in on Paolo's accusation that a blonde nurse had been going through her papers. She hesitated to get Sergeant Meyers into trouble, but she could question him herself to see if it might be his girl who was the culprit.

"That's a serious problem," Major Rosenbach said. "I'm sorry I didn't pay more attention earlier. We'll have the guards keep a sharp eye out."

Evie thanked him, but it didn't feel like enough. She didn't want to wait for the nurse to come to her. She wanted to find the woman before she did more damage. Sergeant Meyers wouldn't take it well if she accused him directly. She had to be more subtle than that.

Evie finished her rounds with Lieutenant Mead and took notes for Major Rosenbach before she had any free time. Then she had to tell...

Who? She could talk to Private Smith and Corporal Higa, but they weren't mobile enough to help her. She needed Glenn, Terry, and Ray. And that meant she needed to make peace with them. With Glenn. Life was too short—too precious—to stay angry.

She found Glenn bouncing a ping pong off the wall.

"Private Holbrook?"

"Miss Lewis?"

"I'm sorry for the things I said. I know you do take things seriously."

He set down the ping pong paddle. "Maybe I don't when I should. Maybe if I'd been more serious, I wouldn't have been wounded. I wouldn't have lost friends in the fighting. I'm always going to wonder. I'm always going to think some of it was my fault."

"I know," Evie said. "My little brother Robbie…" She paused. She didn't usually dredge up this dark fear, and the words came slowly. "He can't enlist because of me. I brought home polio from a friend's house. I got better from it, but it left him with one leg twisted and shorter than the other. He doesn't blame me—at least not out loud—but I can't help thinking that if it weren't for me, he'd have a normal life."

"You couldn't have helped that."

"You couldn't have helped that there was a war going on."

"But we still blame ourselves," Glenn said.

Evie nodded. Of course, if it weren't for the polio, maybe Robbie would have been in a plane that went down over India too. She squeezed her eyes against the tears.

"Miss Lewis?"

"I got a telegram. They found the wreckage of Albert's plane."

Glenn was quiet for a long moment. Then, he wrapped her in his arms, and she sobbed into his shoulder. After she wiped her eyes, she said, "I'm sorry."

"Don't be. I'm sorry about your brother."

"I'm going to do this for him. Paolo told me he saw a nurse going through the papers on my desk. Not one of the nurses in our ward."

"Could he say who it was?"

"No, just that she had very light blonde hair and was pretty, but he says everyone is pretty."

"Hey, he's never called me pretty."

Evie smiled and shook her head. "You know, that tech sergeant down in the lab…" she hesitated. She had promised not

97

to tell, but this was important. "There's a nurse he's friendly with. She's a platinum blonde."

"There are a lot of blonde nurses at Bushnell."

"But at least we could ask."

He shrugged. "Okay."

They made their way down to the lab, and Evie caught the tech sergeant's eye. He flushed a little and shooed her out, hurrying to meet her in the hallway.

"What's this?" he asked.

"I wondered if the nurse who returned my missing file to you had very light blonde hair."

Sergeant Meyers frowned. "She did. Why?"

"Was she the nurse you were... friends with?"

The sergeant gave Glenn a wary look and said, "Well, I guess it doesn't matter, because she won't see me anymore. Yeah, it was the same girl. She seemed so interested, and then..."

"After the penicillin disappeared, she dropped you?" Glenn asked.

The tech sergeant didn't say anything, but the redness of his face gave him away.

"What was her name?" Evie asked.

"Carol Browning," the tech sergeant muttered. "Now, if you'll excuse me."

Glenn and Evie looked at each other.

"Is that enough to get her?" Glenn asked.

"Let's tell Major Rosenbach," Evie said.

They found the doctor getting ready to leave for the day. He frowned at them. "Miss Lewis?"

"Sir, we think we know who was going through my desk, and who took the penicillin."

"The penicillin?"

"The medicine that was supposed to be for Jeannie Harding's baby. We think it was stolen by a nurse named Carol Browning."

"That's a serious charge."

"She matches the description that Paolo—the POW—gave, and she was fraternizing with a lab technician, but as soon as the penicillin disappeared, so did she."

"Hmm. Very well, that sounds convincing. I'll report it and see what we can find out."

But when he returned a short time later, his face was grim.

"Are you certain the name was Carol Browning?"

"That's what the lab technician told us."

"We may have to turn him in to be questioned."

"Why?"

"There's no Carol Browning working at Bushnell—not as a nurse or anything else."

"A spy?" Evie asked.

"It's possible. You did a good thing uncovering this, Miss Lewis."

"Thank you, sir." Evie said.

But it didn't feel like a good thing. The spy got away, and so did the penicillin.

"You're still dissatisfied?" Glenn asked her a couple of days later as she played cards with him, Terry, Ray, and Corporal Higa. Christmas music blared from the radio Higa had made in the electronics shop, and Terry was smoking his last cigarette as a

Bushnell patient. He was wearing his dressy arms for the trip home—the ones that looked real but didn't function as well as the hook hands.

"She's still out there. Maybe she's reporting back to Hitler, and she'll be back at some other hospital to steal something else."

"You did everything you could, Miss Lewis."

"I know, but I came so close."

They played on in silence. Paolo strolled by, waving hi as he cleaned the windows. Music came from out in the hallway—a choir singing. College girls often came to entertain the wounded troops, and around Christmas time, a constant stream of carolers roamed up and down the halls. Evie traded in a three for an ace and glanced up in passing to see the choir stream into the ward, all wearing nurses' uniforms. Several of the boys stopped what they were doing to watch the nurses singing to them.

Across the room, Paolo was staring at Evie, making an excited gesture with his hands. Evie scrunched her forehead, then her eyes widened. One of the nurses had hair so blonde it was almost white.

"Glenn?" she asked.

"Yeah?" he whispered.

"I think Paolo's telling us the nurse he saw is here singing to us."

"What, she didn't leave?"

"Apparently not!"

"What do we do?" Glenn motioned to get his friends' attention.

"We have to get close enough to stop her from running then alert Major Rosenbach."

"You hear that, boys?" Corporal Higa whispered. "Flanking maneuvers."

He whispered some commands to the men, who casually repositioned themselves until they were fanned out around the nurses. Evie slipped through the crowd, going for Major Rosenbach. The platinum blonde stopped singing for a moment and watched her passing, but Evie tried not to glance in her direction.

"Major Rosenbach," she whispered, attracting his attention from the nurses. "Paolo says the nurse is in this group of singers. The platinum blonde."

"I'll call a guard. They can handle questioning her."

He slipped out of the room. Evie turned back to watch the singers. The platinum blonde had worked her way to the back of the group, and she was casting glances at the door. She caught Evie's eyes and ran.

Evie bolted forward, but the nurse had a head start. Terry darted around the choir and caught up with the nurse, fumbling after her.

The blonde woman batted his hands away and shrieked. She threw something into the air. Terry's false arm. It caught in the garlands over the doorway.

That stopped the singing, and some of the soldiers laughed at the sight of Terry with one of his arms gone, the other dangling from the decorations. The nurse kept running, and more of the men laughed, mistaking her real reason for fleeing.

Private Smith lunged after her from his bed but missed and rolled to the floor. Glenn stopped to catch him. Corporal Higa charged his wheelchair forward, and the choir scattered. He rammed into the back of the blonde's legs and sent her sprawling.

Evie pounced, pinning the woman down and calling for the guards.

The patients and nurses gathered in a wide-eyed circle. Two uniformed guards ran up to find Evie and the nurse flat on the floor.

"She's been stealing penicillin!" Evie said.

"That's not true!" the woman yelped. "Get off me!"

Paolo pushed his way forward and pointed. "Is bad lady. Steals papers. I see."

"Talk to Sergeant Meyers down in the lab," Evie said to the guards. "I think he'll be able to corroborate our story."

The guards nodded and hauled the woman away.

Several days later, Glenn read to everyone from the latest edition of the *Bugle*.

"Well, that confirms it," he said.

"What?" Ray asked.

"We didn't win the Christmas decorating contest this year. I knew we should have used more mistletoe."

Everyone groaned.

"Get on with the real news!" Ray said.

"Lieutenant Carol *Nelson* was taken into custody for stealing penicillin from the hospital labs. She was using it to treat her sick mother."

The group fell quiet.

"It's hard to fault her for that," Private Smith said.

"But it was still stealing from other people who needed it." Glenn snapped the newspaper closed.

"They got another shipment of penicillin," Evie said. "Jeannie's baby is recovering well from her surgery."

That was met by nods of approval all around. Corporal Higa struck up another Christmas song on his guitar, and they all joined in singing "Silent Night." Paolo warbled along in Italian and danced with his mop.

"I got you an early Christmas present," Glenn said to Evie under the strains of the songs.

He handed her a Milky Way bar. She hesitated, giving him a wary look.

"I think your brother would want you to enjoy it for him."

Evie nodded and took the candy, her eyes stinging. Outside, a light dusting of snow made the mountains glow pink in the sunset. A distant whistle announced the arrival of another train at Bushnell. They would be busy again soon, but at that moment, in their ward, everything was at peace. Evie slowly peeled the wax paper wrapper off the candy bar and took a bite, enjoying the sensation of sinking her teeth through the soft nougat and sweet chocolate. The caramel melted on her tongue. She sat next to Glenn in silence while she ate, soaking in the bright colors of the sunset, the familiar tunes of the ancient carols, and the warmth of being with friends.

"Thank you," Evie said.

"I don't suppose..." Glenn cleared his throat. "I don't suppose you'd like to go out some time? I know they ask you to flirt with us fellows, but I thought, maybe..."

Evie shook her head. "I can't."

Glenn nodded quickly. "Of course. I understand. It just would have been for fun, after all. You know, to practice—"

Evie put her hand on his. "I'm not allowed to date patients. But I hear you'll be released soon, and then it's a different matter."

His eyes brightened. "Really?"

She smiled and nodded.

"I really should have used more mistletoe."

She laughed. "Not until after you walk out of here."

"I'll tell them to move my release date up a couple of weeks. I just got really motivated."

Evie laughed and kept her hand on Glenn's, comforted by the warmth of his touch. That, at least, she didn't have to wait for.

A nurse hurried up to Evie, breaking the spell. "Miss Lewis? They want you down at the train depot. I guess one of the new patients was asking for you, said he might know something about what happened to your brother."

Evie's chest tightened, and she looked at Glenn. Did she want to know whatever this soldier had to tell her about Albert?

"Go," he said giving her hand a heartening squeeze.

Evie hurried out of the ward and jogged down the hallways, dodging carolers and trying not to get tangled in the strands of Christmas lights painting the halls in bright reds and greens. At least she might get some answers now. Or would this only bring more questions?

The night air in the train station was icy, but it felt good on Evie's cheeks after her run. Orderlies carried patients out of the train on stretchers. Evie searched each face. How would she know which one?

"Evie!"

She glanced up in surprise to see Robbie waving to her. He limped forward, leaning on his cane.

"Robbie!" She flung her arms around him, realizing the nurse hadn't said which brother. "Are you hurt?"

He smiled and motioned to one of the stretchers. Evie's heartbeat picked up, and it was suddenly hard to breathe. She slowly came forward to look down at the stretcher. A familiar face beamed up at her.

"Albert!" She fell to her knees and threw her arms around her brother.

"Careful, Sis! They got all the shrapnel out, but I've still got a way to go."

"Oh my gosh, what happened? We thought..." She choked on the words, tears of fear and joy stinging her eyes.

"I know. I survived the crash and crawled back until I found some friendly locals to take me in. I was hurt pretty bad and in-and-out for a long time before I could tell them who to ask for help. By that time, my leg was too far gone to infection."

Evie took his hand. "But you're alive! And you're in the right place now. You'll be playing basketball with the other boys in no time. And just in time for Christmas." Evie looked from Albert to Robbie. "Do Mom and Dad know?"

"I sent them a telegram as soon as I got to California," Albert said, "but when I found out I was coming to Bushnell, I decided to surprise you. I bet the folks will be here by tomorrow morning."

Evie reached blindly for Robbie's hand and squeezed it. "We'll all be together for Christmas again!"

Hopefully Fran didn't mind crowding her whole family onto the floor of their room. There certainly wasn't space anywhere else in Brigham City.

"I brought you something." Albert held up a Milky Way bar.

Evie laughed, and fresh tears rolled down her cheeks. "Oh, Albert."

"You have to share it with Robbie," he said. "Maybe we'll wait for Christmas to open it. Something to look forward to. It'll be a real holiday to remember!"

"Yes." Evie grinned through her tears. "But right now is perfect too."

Author's Note

Bushnell General Military Hospital operated in Brigham City, Utah from 1942 to 1946, treating over 10,000 men with amputations, PTSD, and other serious injuries from World War II. Though the events in this novella are fictional, they are based on some real events.

Bushnell was the first hospital to experiment with penicillin, and it was at Bushnell that the "Wonder Drug" first proved itself. The trials weren't secret, but the results were kept out of print at first, probably to keep the information out of enemy hands. Through most of the war, penicillin remained in high demand, mostly for military use, though by the end of the war it was available for some civilians as well. It gave the Allies a distinct advantage over the Axis powers, who were still relying on older, less-effective sulfa drugs to treat infections.

Helen Keller was one of many celebrities who visited Bushnell, and though I don't have a transcript of her speech, what she said inspired the patients at the hospital to feel that their troubles were lighter. She did sing along with the piano by feeling the vibrations.

There was also a Christmas baby born at Bushnell who was saved by a hernia surgery, but I have modified her story somewhat to fit the novella and protect the privacy of someone who may still be living.

The story of the secretary noticing that a spy had been going through her papers actually happened a little further south, at the Defense Depot in Ogden, Utah, but I moved it to Bushnell for the sake of the story.

The newspaper at Bushnell was called the *Bugle*, and it provided me with details like the Christmas decorating contest and the mirrors being installed at intersections to prevent accidents. I imagine at least one run-in like Glenn and Evie's must have occurred if they saw the need for the mirrors. It's also easy to imagine the young soldiers with their wheelchairs racing in the halls and otherwise making the best of their situation. Though there was a great deal of suffering at Bushnell, visitors often commented on the positive attitude of the patients there.

A POW branch camp was located just south of Bushnell. It first housed Italian and then German POWs. The POWs weren't supposed to socialize with the patients or employees at Bushnell, but they often tried to flirt with the girls (even when they knew little or no English), and some of them formed close friendships with the patients. The story of the POW sneaking out for a night on the town in a borrowed American uniform actually occurred at Bushnell with a German POW.

Bushnell was also interesting for being unsegregated at a time when the military and most of American society was segregated. Bushnell was the general hospital for the West Coast—and especially for amputee patients—so soldiers from California, the Southwest, the Pacific Northwest, and Hawaii recovered there, representing a wide spectrum of ethnic groups. This included quite a few of the Japanese-American soldiers who had fought with the famous 442nd Regimental Combat Team made up entirely of Japanese Americans, many of who had been incarcerated in internment camps before volunteering to serve their country. The 442nd was the most decorated unit of World War II, but Japanese Americans (including the community in Utah) still faced prejudice at home.

I have attempted to portray Bushnell accurately, at least the outline of it. If you want to know more about Bushnell Hospital or Utah during the war years, I recommend the following resources:

"Bushnell Days" online exhibit from Utah State University, http://exhibits.usu.edu/exhibits/show/bushnelldays

Andrea Kaye Carter, "Bushnell General Military Hospital and the Community of Brigham City"

Allan Kent Powell, *Utah Remembers World War II*

Allan Kent Powell, *Splinters of a Nation: German Prisoners of War in Utah*

"Utah World War II Stories," oral histories collected by KUED, https://www.kued.org/whatson/kued-productions/utah-world-war-ii-stories

If you're interested in learning more about Evie's parents' experience in Utah during World War I, check out my novel *No Peace with the Dawn*, available online from Amazon, Kobo, Google Play Books, and Barnes & Noble, and through major retailers including Barnes & Noble, Deseret Book, Target, and Walmart.

If you enjoyed this book, please remember to rate it on Amazon. Thank you!

Acknowledgements

Thank you to the many people who helped make this book possible. Britney, Dan, Jeff, Karen, Lauren, and Sherrie Lynn gave invaluable feedback. The archives at Utah State University, Weber State University, the University of Utah, Brigham Young University, Brigham City Library, the National Library of Medicine, and the National Museum of Health and Medicine provided pictures and oral history interviews that helped me piece together an understanding of Bushnell Hospital, though any errors or omissions are my own. And as always, I couldn't do this without the support of my wonderful family.

About the Author

E.B. WHEELER attended BYU, majoring in history with an English minor, and earned graduate degrees in history and landscape architecture from Utah State University. She's the award-winning author of *The Haunting of Springett Hall*, Whitney Award finalist *Born to Treason*, *No Peace with the Dawn* (with Jeffery Bateman), and *Yours, Dorothy*, as well as several short stories, magazine articles, and scripts for educational software programs. She was named the 2016 Writer of the Year by the League of Utah Writers. In addition to writing, she consults about historic preservation and teaches history at USU.

You can find her online at www.ebwheeler.com

To find out about new releases and special deals, subscribe to her newsletter at http://eepurl.com/bqCKTr